CHIMES AT MIDNIGHT

CHIMES AT MIDNIGHT

Twelve Stories

by

TERENCE de VERE WHITE

LONDON
VICTOR GOLLANCZ LTD
1977

29300

ISBN 0 575 02290 6

MADE AND PRINTED IN GREAT BRITAIN BY
THE GARDEN CITY PRESS LIMITED
LETCHWORTH, HERTFORDSHIRE
SG6 1JS

CONTENTS

VERY LIKE A WHALE

SHE HAD PERSISTED characteristically down the
long, narrow, unpromising lane, and now the sea came into
view. Her little eyes shone with triumph and she began to
drive dangerously fast; the lane, which had deteriorated,
became a sheep track, and it ended indecisively in a field of
short rank grass. Charlotte abandoned her motor car and
went forward on foot. Where the track ended there was a
hollow; the sea was invisible from there, but she could hear it
plunge and sigh, and gulls complaining somewhere close at
hand. She ran up the bank—a small puffing wobbling figure
with a pain in her side—and then she saw the whale.

It lay on its side less than a hundred yards out to sea,
motionless, wavelets lapping its sides, crawling up and
slithering over it, while gulls flew round in watchful
attendance. A whale : Charlotte laughed aloud. This was
something to tell Francis. He would say one of his funny
things—all Charlotte's whales are rocks. Making fun of her,
but she didn't mind. At least he would be paying her
attention. She sat down to rest. She was in a sweat. What a
day to choose to run up a hill ! She never ran, never walked,
if it came to that, unless she had to. Would she ever get back
her breath again ?

Then a tentative breeze came stealing off the sea and
passed sweetly over her clammy skin. She lay back and closed
her eyes. The wind was like an angel's kiss. It was delicious.
Francis had kissed her once. Seven years ago. He was rather
drunk at the time. He said she was good and deserved love.
She had worshipped him ever since.

When she woke up the whale had gone. The sea presented

a smooth flat unwrinkled surface of blues and greys and greens on which the sun danced. She had been dreaming.

She got up feeling heavy-eyed and stupid; her skirt and blouse stuck to her uncomfortably. For a moment she had no idea where she was or how she had got there. Then she remembered a lane that she had never seen before, although she had driven along the north road scores of times; she knew it had already been decided that she was to turn into that lane; there was something at the end of it for her. A rock that looked very like a whale!

Now she took sober stock of her surroundings. As far as she could see fields of poor grass, like the one she was in, stretched along the coast. Beneath her there was a cove of clean firm sand; it ended at a projecting headland. Charlotte made her way down the bank to the strand; she was curious to see what was on the other side of the head. She was big with a sense of adventure. All roads in her thoughts led to Francis. But she would not have had him with her now. He would make her feel inadequate. He was for ever tossing up balloons of fancy, allegedly for her entertainment, but they only exposed her awkwardness when she tried to catch them. What she liked best of all to do was to go exploring like this in her own way and then, when she was quite sure she had discovered something worthy of his notice, to introduce it to Francis. She would then be in control of the situation. She had to have ten yards' start, as it were, if she were to race him on anything like even terms. Not that she thought of her relationship with Francis as a race. A race takes two; and he never moved at all. But he was always there.

He, too, remembered that kiss. It had been a match dropped by a drunken man in a careless moment on parched grass. He had been paying for the damage by instalments ever since. The gifts laid on the altar of this god—rich because the worshipper was well-to-do—changed their character as soon as he beheld them from silk, gold, ivory, tortoiseshell, finest leather to IOU's, promises to pay, extended indefinitely. Even now Charlotte was collecting a view for him, a place to come for a picnic (what sweet trouble she would go to preparing for it).

The strand came to an abrupt end. It was now a question whether she could paddle round the corner of the cliff on the sea side or clamber up its uncomfortable face and approach what lay behind it overland. She should not have come down when she did. She took off her shoes and stockings, held up her skirt, and consigned herself to the sea. In fact the water never came up to her thighs, but she moved cautiously, not trusting the element. When she looked up she was round the corner; facing her were her cottages.

'Her cottages' she called them, because it was revealed to her at once that this row of ruins was what her steps had been guided to find. They could almost certainly be bought for a song and put into repair by a local builder. Charlotte may not have had looks or brilliant intelligence, but she had quite a lot of money. And it would not have surprised anyone who knew her to discover that when she was thinking with one layer of her mind that this would be the perfect site for the installation of Francis, with the other she was calculating the expense involved and deciding that the shares in the brewery would realise about the amount required. A love nest and an investment with what her stockbroker called 'growth potential'—her conscience would be at ease.

The cottages knocked together would provide all the needed accommodation. There would have to be several bedrooms because—and with the thought Charlotte's face became startlingly like an angry pig's—Francis would never come down alone. James would have to be included in the party. It did not need to be spoken. And James would want to bring his new girl. Not that Charlotte had any objection to that. If only James and one of his girls would get out from under Francis's shadow—then the situation might change. Francis might need her then.

Now she was in one of her fussy moods. She got like this whenever she had gone to endless trouble to please Francis and either he didn't notice or let all her careful preparations go to waste. She was always in charge; having to concentrate while Francis sauntered along laughing with James when she was serious, or talking above her head when she wasn't.

When Charlotte had a thought, she translated it into action at once. Already she was looking about her for someone to tell her about the cottages. If it were possible, she would have bought them on the spot. They lined a sloping path, and behind them was another lane, rather more substantial than the one that she had come down. It, too, must lead back to the road. She remembered catching a glimpse of a petrol station when she turned into the lane. That is where she would probably get the information she wanted. Excited, determined, wholly concentrated; from the back as she moved quickly (overland this time)—head down, tail swaying—with her short legs, a basset hound on the scent.

The petrol station consisted of a cottage which was used as a shop for the sale of cigarettes and sweets. There was a petrol pump at the side, and today an old man was in charge of the lot.

Charlotte began her business by buying as much petrol as her car's tank would hold; then, because it seemed more natural to talk indoors, she made a ceremony of buying mixed sweets. It was not simply a ruse. She was over-fond of sweets and grateful for the excuse.

"I'll have a quarter of a pound of those jellies, and, let me see . . ."

The old man went from one jar to another, pausing at each while Charlotte decided what measure she would buy. "And quarter of a pound of mixed chocolates." With that she completed the purchase.

She had taken out her road map, and she invited the shop man to show her exactly where they were. He took the map from her and inexpertly began to run a finger down the coast from a point about fifty miles north. "Somewhere there." Charlotte could never let that sort of incompetence pass unreproved, even if it made a man thankful that he wasn't married to her.

She didn't need this assistance, but it was a way of involving him in her enterprise. She didn't mention the cottages at first. She was not going to show her hand to that extent.

"That's a beautiful beach. I never knew of its existence before."

"People don't know about it because there's no proper road. There's another nice beach further on."

"Where the rock is."

"Aye, the whale rock we call it, but you'd want to be careful if you're swimming. It's dangerous in the channel at the turn of the tide. A brother of mine got himself drownded there. I haven't been next or near it since I was a child. But the other beach is safe. You could walk half-way to Wales before the water would be up to your knees."

"Who owns the cottages on this side of the cliff?"

"Do you mean where the Coast Guard Station used to be? That was destroyed in the Troubles and the cottages were let fall into ruin. Nobody could live in them now. They're useful for shelter."

"They are Government property, then."

"I suppose so. A man called Carty owns all the land round there. You'll pass his house if you're going back to Dublin. The first gate on the left."

Charlotte changed the conversation then, and discussed the prospects of war in Europe. But briefly; she was eager to begin her great campaign.

She had no intention of calling on Mr Carty who would probably resent her intrusion. Coast Guard property would certainly be under the control of the Board of Works, in which her cousin Alfred was an engineer. She might call on Alfred that very afternoon. It was curious, she reflected as she drove homeward, that someone belonging to such an eminently practical family as she did, and who was so practical herself, should be attracted by anyone so gloriously helpless in practical matters as Francis was. Couldn't boil an egg, much less drive a car. Hopelessly dependent. It was lovely, of course, for her. When James wasn't available—sometimes he went on circuit and was away for days at a time; and there were evenings when he took this girl of his and her several predecessors out to dine or dance and God knows what else—then Francis, if he hadn't enough work to distract his mind, would get lonely and ring up (knowing Charlotte was sitting beside the telephone) and her antennae would be all a-quiver to catch a need. Had he mentioned a corn, she would have been over to cut it for him straight away. He never, in fact, mentioned corns; but the radio might be giving trouble or a light have fused or he might have suddenly decided to go out when James was not there to drive him—those were the moments when Charlotte came into her own.

Sometimes, of course, his complacency exacerbated her. "I give, give, give," she told herself bitterly, and what did she get in return? But the hardest blow would have been Francis's refusal to take, take, take. And he was always charming, if sometimes careless. He was so used to getting his way. Too strong a personality. He dominated their lives, not only Charlotte's (who lived for nothing else), but James would have married that Peggy girl if he wasn't so completely under Francis's thumb. She was obviously dotty about him, but he was taking his time, afraid, if the truth were known, of asserting himself. Francis's possessiveness was very difficult to combat. He didn't contest with rivals; he absorbed them, acting like some international cartel that takes over a going concern including the managers. Francis and James and Peggy (people couldn't always remember her name) were to be seen together at restaurants and theatres, at the races. Francis playing host and being delightful to Peggy. They were going to Vienna in September. Charlotte fortunately had the sort of skin that doesn't flush or she would have betrayed her agony when she heard about this.

She had striven so hard (giving, giving, giving) to make them into a foursome, a square dance; but they, ungratefully, appeared to regard themselves as a trio and self-sufficient unless she took the initiative. Then they acquiesced, and included her.

The cottages were what promised to bring about the situation that to Charlotte was so obviously the logical one. Here they would be together under her roof. And the cottages could always be let if they had plans to go away together. Why if Francis was prepared to accept James's girls could he not include Charlotte as well? She would never make a nuisance of herself. On the contrary, she liked better than anything to slave for him. She could see herself preparing elaborate meals in the cottages while James and his girl disported themselves in the sea and Francis looked on—thinking what? He was an enigma. She never knew what he was thinking. It wasn't merely that he was a very brilliant man, intellectual and witty, hard for anyone to keep up with—it was his attitude that she didn't understand. She knew that he must be queer—in the 'thirties in Dublin a girl like Charlotte didn't know much about queers and felt rather over-emancipated when she mentioned them. But if he was queer, then why did he spend so much time with James who was always philandering with women? Didn't queers consort with their own kind? But then she laughed and sighed at herself; here she was laying down the law about queers when her aim in life was to marry the only one she knew. She had read in novels about men who asked girls to marry them, and promised if they did never to ask for anything more. It was the ultimate in selfless devotion. In practice, though, the woman who made such a bargain would be a selfish bitch. If she was being magnanimous, why not go the whole hog? If she wasn't, then what was she up to? Marrying the man for his money? Expecting to take lovers on the side? In fact, in the novels that inspired these reflections, the woman's purity was the crux of the matter. That was what all the fuss was about.

If Francis was to marry her on his terms, then she would have to promise not to bother him. She would be quite ready to do that for the sake of living with him, of seeing him every day. But what if he expected her to allow him to have adventures? She would die of jealousy.

What was his relationship with James? Did he—no, it wasn't possible! She preferred not to think about it. And what did a girl like Peggy think? She, surely, resented Francis's inevitable presence (and when he wasn't there, James's citing him as if he were Sir Oracle). Did James put her mind at ease on the essential matter? That left them in the position of countries whose governments have signed an *entente cordiale*. 'The girl' was a member of the *entente*, even if she had to watch her step and not talk out of turn. Charlotte, after seven years of 'giving, giving, giving', was not inside the *entente* at all, although she made it look sometimes as if she were. (How could she get herself included in the Vienna trip? Offer her car? Ask James to ask Francis? James would be glad to have her there so that he could get off sometimes on his own with Peggy. But Charlotte hated to demean herself to the level of begging favours from James. She despised him—a water-colour reproduction of his friend. But younger and better looking, if one were to disregard Francis's authority and presence and concentrate on outline and surfaces.) But in Vienna she would not show to her best advantage. She would read it up, of course, beforehand, thoroughly, so as not to be made look a fool in front of James and that girl of his. She didn't mind so much when she was alone with Francis. He seemed to expect nothing from her. But having gone to all that trouble she was sure to be made angry and miserable by Francis and James making their tiresome jokes and allusions, treating her like a child; having things offered to her and then held out of reach as a tease. Besides, she hated abroad; she got hot so easily, and she was never able to change her usual topics of conversation because she happened to be travelling. She couldn't change her real interests just like that. At home she was in her own kingdom. That is why the cottages excited her so much. Here she could establish herself attractively. It was so accessible, an hour's drive from Dublin. Not a soul in sight on a day of cracking heat when, along the south coast, the sands at this distance from town would be beetle black with milling hordes.

"Alfred will get them for me." That was her final decision. Having made it, she wouldn't waver. Knowing her own mind, she was prepared to make a nuisance of herself to Alfred and anyone else until she had secured her objective. That is how she got things. That is how she would get Francis. Only a very rich girl could afford to indulge such a fancy. Two thousand pounds would have bought a mansion in spacious grounds at that time, before the Hitler war. Charlotte, in her mind's eye, saw several bathrooms, built-in cupboards, a modern kitchen, a room for Francis to work in with a picture window. Other guests would be isolated in what was now the ruins of the last cottage in the row. They would have their own sitting-room. There would be nothing to compare with it along that coast.

Nothing works out exactly as imagination painted it, even when the desired end seems to be obtained. Other people are unpredictable, for one thing. Charlotte bought the cottages for the expected sum and renovated them. Not to the extent or degree that she had pictured when she made her miraculous discovery. When Francis refused to commit himself to any regular attendance, it was too humiliating to fix the place up for him. He insisted that the scheme was Charlotte's own. She had bought herself a super seaside cottage. But he made it quite clear that he did not intend to install himself at weekends or to change his plan of life. He was ready, of course, to accept invitations or to suggest visits on his own initiative, sometimes to take friends without always letting Charlotte know in advance, to drop in on chance, expecting nothing, he assured her, when she was disconcerted by being taken unawares. Not that she ever was again; she stayed in resolutely with a full larder whenever she was down—as was usually the case—at the cottage without Francis. "Such a waste," her friends used to say. "She sits in the house all day."

When Francis did condescend to come, he was usually driven by James. Sometimes he had to employ other friends because James was not always available. His wooing of Peggy was having a rough passage. She had broken out of the threesome, and was sometimes seen with an actor and sometimes with a young doctor whose motor car was as prominent in the local scene as the Eiffel Tower in Paris. Nobody could be so affluent as that car suggested; and to hear that Peggy was to be seen in it made James unhappy. She spoke of going to Australia where her brother was. Whenever she brought up the subject, James asked her to marry him and she refused. They quarrelled so frequently that an evening with Peggy made James unapproachable for the twenty-four hours following. Whenever he lost his temper she remained cool and asked him if he had ever been told that his voice, for a man, was unusually high-pitched. She became mysterious. "I am sorry I can't," she would say when he issued an invitation. "I promised to go out with someone." So that he was miserable when he was with her, and jealous when he was not.

Francis, too, had changed. He was drinking too much. Charlotte was in a constant dilemma. "God bless you," he used to say when she produced the very best brandy; but she reproached herself for playing on his weakness. One evening she called on him and found he was incapable of talking sense or doing his work. He kissed her. It was the second time, after seven years. He hadn't the least idea what he was doing. His breath stank of brandy. If he went on like this he would be ruined professionally. She had enough to keep them both. He need never want, and there was something in the thought of rescuing him from the gutter that kindled her imagination, the sure knowledge that at last he must take the all she had to give. But it would be better for Francis's sake to cure him of his drinking habit than to use it as the Styx he had to cross to meet her on the lonely shore. She tried to talk to him about it, even to admonish him. He lost his temper. Once he turned on her and said, "I wish you would go away. Why can't you leave me alone? Have you no pride, woman?"

Then she cried bitterly and reproached him for ingratitude.

"But I don't want anything from you," he said. "I only ask to be left in peace."

"I love you," she said. "I can't help it. You made me love you. I didn't ask you to. I never dreamed of it. I'm not to be blamed. I would do anything in the world for you."

"Then, just go away like a decent woman."

"And leave you like this? How can I do that?"

Then Francis would make a violent effort, at some expense to his temper, and abjure all strong liquors. But after a few months, he would fall again. When that happened Charlotte communicated with James who was always aware of the crisis. He repaid the kindness Francis had shown him by taking over as much of his work as he could, and covering his tracks with the sympathetic assistance of others who were concerned to help. Francis was much loved. And there is infinite tolerance of drunkenness in Ireland, as if it were generally conceded that inside every man there was an emotional Sahara. But this state of affairs could not last.

Francis needed help. It was useless to remonstrate with him. James had his own problems with Peggy as well as an increasing practice to absorb his time and energy. He could only help in a crisis. Charlotte was ready and prepared to act as a St Bernard dog; there was nothing that she would ask in life other than this. She said so to James, who did not say that the image was touching but inapt. The sort of dog Francis needed was not one who came to a man lost in the snow with a brandy flask. It would be preferable to die than to live in Charlotte's remorseless care, James told himself, but then, he had no other solution to Francis's problem to offer. He knew all about their history. Francis told him about the first kiss. He would never forgive himself. But surely, James argued, she must have been kissed before by someone.

"She said she had always loved me but never dreamt that I would deign to notice her. I do remember that she looked miserably unhappy at dances. She was often without a partner. I can't remember how I came to be taking her home, but I suppose her misery touched me, and I wanted to do something to relieve it, and I could only think of kissing her and saying something to cheer her up. Do you remember that poor novel with the wonderful title, *Beware of Pity*? I always think of that when I see Charlotte. Because I kissed her once out of pity, I must kiss her until I die unless I am prepared to do her a worse hurt."

James thought that his friend was excessively conscientious, and saw Charlotte as one of the most ruthless characters he had ever encountered; but he wasn't free to say so. That was what happened when he came under Francis's influence. He lost the power of independent action. When he talked about Peggy to Francis, he listened sympathetically. "If you want my advice you should rape her," he said.

Another time, speculating about Tunis—where he had never been—Francis suggested that they should go there for James's honeymoon. James had lacked the courage to say he didn't relish the idea of Francis's company on that trip. If and when the time came he knew he would be locked in indecision whether to see how Peggy would take it (so as not to hurt Francis's feelings) or to try to muster up courage to tell Francis that Peggy wouldn't like it. And if he did that, Francis was quite capable of asking Peggy whether or not this was true; whereupon she would turn on James for having put the blame on her.

"We are too considerate, that's our trouble," James said to Francis, but secretly he thought Francis was weak not to have given Charlotte her walking papers long since.

Since Francis's drinking problem, always latent, had so drastically surfaced, James was grateful enough that

Charlotte was there. He found he could talk to her. He thought she liked him for Francis's sake.

One day when James was moping in his flat, having been out with Peggy on the previous evening, a ring at the door sent him flying with a frantic hope to answer it. He could not prevent his face from falling when he saw Charlotte standing there, like a sentry. As she rarely raised a smile by her advent, she may not have noticed. Charlotte wasted no time on the examination of nuances. She knew no intermediate shades between black and white. Having decided to come to a final conclusion about Francis, she wasted no time, and announced her purpose at once.

"I'm going to propose," she said. "My mother told me once that no nice man ever proposed; it was always the woman. I'm doing it anyway. If Francis isn't taken care of he is going to be ruined and he is going to die. I want to tell you this—I feel I should—I know all about Francis. But I don't know exactly what there is between him and you. And I want to say this : it is up to you to keep out of Francis's way. I'm not throwing stones; I'm thinking only of him. I don't give a damn what happens to me or what happens to you. But I'll have enough to cope with, without having to cope with you. Why don't you marry Peggy?"

"It's not my fault. I've asked her to often enough."

"She was crazy about you."

"I never noticed it."

"You were too much impressed by Francis. I don't blame her if she has cold feet about marrying you. No girl wants to give herself to a man who is under someone's influence to the extent you are under Francis's. Apart from anything else."

"There never was 'anything else' as you put it between Francis and me."

"That's no business of mine. I'm only concerned with the future."

"I swear it. Ask Francis. Have you ever suggested this to Peggy? Someone has been at her. I'm sure of it."

"She doesn't need anyone to get *at* her. Anyhow, this is your opportunity. Tell her I'm marrying Francis and you've been forbidden the house. And if I were you I'd do something to prove it to the girl that you were a man."

"Have you been talking to Francis about me?"

"No. I've better things to talk to him about."

"Asking him to marry you, for instance."

"I never did."

"Forgive me, please. I'm sorry for saying that; but you shouldn't have talked as you did about Peggy and me. Anyhow, I've told you the truth."

And then Charlotte began to cry. She looked so hideous that James felt a sudden rush of sympathy for her. By one remark he had revealed that he knew what had passed between Francis and herself, that this great resolve was in fact a decision to use force to obtain what she had begged for until he had become too weak to resist.

"Just because he's ... It doesn't mean he can't ... When I think ..."

James patted her gently on the back. He could think of nothing else to do. She wished him dead.

As soon as she recovered herself, Charlotte asked for leave to use the bathroom. She emerged after a long absence looking reconditioned. She was always very puffy round the eyes. But Francis was unlikely to scrutinise her closely. She was fit for her task.

"Good luck," James said. She made no reply. She had forgotten his existence. She was on the scent.

When Charlotte rang at the door of Francis's flat he did not rush to answer it; but when he did he smiled when he saw her standing to attention in the doorway.

He had a ravishing smile.

"I was just about to pick up the telephone when you came just now, Charlotte. It just shows how perfect is the telepathy between us. I wanted to find out if there was the least chance of your ever agreeing to marry me."

* * *

Charlotte's engagement appeared in the newspaper two days after Francis's proposal. In the same column on the same day, Peggy's parents announced their pleasure at her engagement to Dermot Hanbury Wilmot Scott. James took it very badly. "We must do what we can to cheer the old boy up," Francis said. "I've asked him to come to the cottages for the weekend."

Charlotte listened as she listened to everything Francis said.

James came down on his own. He looked tired but otherwise well enough. During lunch Francis told him about his proposal to Charlotte in minutest detail.

"Don't look so coy, old woman," he said. "You accepted me at once. Don't listen to her James if she tries to pretend she didn't."

After lunch they took books and went walking, looking for some place where they could find shade, out of the wind. To Charlotte's annoyance there was a large party of what looked like orphans with two nuns in attendance on the beach.

"If this place is going to be ruined by trippers I'll sell it," she said.

"What's round the corner?" Francis enquired. "I've never had the energy to look."

They walked along in silence, the three of them; Charlotte holding Francis's left arm in hers. He put out his right and laid it on James's shoulder, nodding at the same time to Charlotte to draw her in and include her in his gesture.

"There's my whale," Charlotte said.

The sea had gone away, except in the place where it ran in a channel beside a large rock about thirty yards in length which looked at if it had been left behind by the tide.

"More like a capsized ship than a whale, I'd say." James hadn't spoken till now.

"Very like a whale," Francis exclaimed, striking a theatrical pose. Charlotte smiled for the first time since lunch. But the smile froze on her face when James said, "Methinks it is like a weasel," and Francis replied, "It is backed like a weasel."

Then he wasn't supporting her. He was talking above her head to James. She was used to it. She was always left out of the conversation.

"Whatever it is," Francis said, noticing Charlotte's displeasure and at a loss to diagnose the cause, "let's make use of it. If we go round the other side, we won't have to go through the water."

The whale or ship or weasel provided exactly the shelter they needed. Francis sat down under the rock and opened his book. Charlotte sat beside him, but she didn't read. James moved about like a dog that wants to bury a bone, looking for a place to settle. He had decided to sunbathe on the far side of the rock. Charlotte half-closed her eyes; Francis looked up sometimes to smile at her. The afternoon slipped quietly away. A church bell ringing the Angelus somewhere in the distance woke Charlotte from a doze. She sat up and looked at Francis, who was sound asleep. His book had fallen on the sand.

When they came there after lunch, the strand looked as if it reached to the horizon; now there was sea everywhere except on the shelf upon which the rock lay. It was still possible to paddle back to land at one point, but at any moment the sea threatened with a scythe-like sweep to cut that off. Charlotte shook Francis's shoulder.

"I must have fallen asleep," he said, rocking his head violently.

"Come quickly. We are going to be cut off by the tide." She bent down and removed his shoes and socks.

"Where did James get to?"

"He must have gone back long ago. This way. Hurry." The water was over their knees. The tide was racing in now.

"We must have been asleep for hours," Francis said. "That place is a death-trap. Did you see the current?"

When they arrived back at the cottages, Charlotte went

into the kitchen to get dinner ready. She was opening a tin when Francis came in looking anxious.

"I wonder where James has got to. I can't find him anywhere."

"Did you look in his room?"

"He wasn't there, and he hasn't taken the car. I looked all along the beach on both sides of the head. I'm desperately worried. What exactly did he say to you? Can you remember?"

"I just heard him moving off. I was half asleep."

"But are you sure he did move off? If you were half asleep you may have only dreamt it."

"You saw for yourself he wasn't there."

"I didn't look on the far side of the rock. You sounded so confident."

He waited for her to say something. She was very carefully opening the tin.

"For God's sake, leave that thing alone," he shouted.

"Why don't you go back to the rock then?"

"Will you come with me?"

"I'll come."

He half-walked, half-ran, and she trotted beside him. She knew he was too weak to face his mounting fear. He needed her now.

OTHELLO'S OCCUPATION

W HEN HE SHUT the door and turned the television on loud, the clatter from the kitchen was muffled. It sounded now like the distant rumble of cannon. He did this in self-defence because he could not believe that it was necessary to create such a din with the dishes for any other reason than to make him feel guilty. He had offered to help when he came in; but she told him he could best do so by keeping out of her way, after she had curtailed his coming-in kiss, saying she hadn't time for that sort of thing just then.

The Wards had been invited to dinner at half-past seven; it was after seven now. Anthea would have to hurry if she was going to make it in time. He heard her come out of the kitchen and go into the bedroom. Then she came out of the bedroom and went into the bathroom, locking the door. She had never done this before yesterday. Perhaps that was why the click of the bolt sounded hostile.

She came into the sitting-room ten minutes after the time fixed for dinner. As the Wards hadn't arrived, it didn't matter. She was looking extremely elegant.

"Oh, have you not even put the drinks out!"

There was mild despair in her voice. Resenting her manner, he set about the task with an injured air.

"It doesn't take all that long," he muttered.

When he had finished she said, "We need ice and lemon."

Brian, unrepentant, looked for ice in the refrigerator and cut his thumb slicing a nasty-looking greenish lemon. He came back then and put the blood-stained lemon on the tray with the glasses.

"Do we need that thing on quite so loud?" She indicated

the television without looking at it. Brian switched off the gardening talk. Silence fell on the room.

"I didn't change," he said.

"So I noticed."

"If they don't like me as I am, they can lump it so far as I am concerned."

"I wonder if it would be too much trouble to pour me out a little whiskey.... I said a *little*." Brian had filled up half a tumbler.

"I'd go easy with that," she said when he put it aside and poured less into another tumbler.

This was a reference to his having got drunk at the party at which this evening's dinner was arranged.

"Look here, Anthea, if you are going to insult me I'll go out and leave you to entertain your friends yourself. I didn't invite them."

"I was only drawing attention to the amount in that tumbler. It would fell an ox."

"Anthea, *please*."

In pouring back some of the excess into the decanter, he let whiskey fall on the polished table. It was Anthea's table. Everything in the room was hers except the turtle-neck sweater, soiled flannel trousers and thick-soled shoes Brian was wearing. And she had given him the sweater, for casual wear.

Anthea got up, went into the kitchen, returned with a cloth, mopped up the whiskey, went back to the kitchen, and then came in again and settled down on the sofa. She sat with her legs up, reading the back pages of the *New Statesman*, feeling for her tumbler so as not to have to take her eyes off the page. Without looking up she said, "Where's the book?"

"What book?"

"You know very well."

"I don't know what you are talking about."

"Tony's novel was on that table. I put it there myself, half an hour ago."

"Oh, *that*."

"Will you please put it back."

"I saw it lying there, but it looked absurd. A dentist doesn't leave false teeth out on the table when his colleagues come to dinner."

"Where did you put it?"

"Where books ought to be, in the bookcase. Don't worry, he will run his eye along the shelves, and nobody could miss that green, white and orange cover."

Anthea got up then and put the book back on the table.

"You've no idea how naïve it makes you look. One would think that you had never met an author in your life before."

"I haven't met many."

"Thanks!"

"Why do you say that?"

"Say what?"

"What are you thanking me for?"

"If you can't see it, I can't explain it. I'll only say this, I think you are being bloody insulting to me."

Anthea knitted her brow; she was acting; he knew when she was acting now. It was like looking at pictures and seeing nothing but chemical colours on canvas.

"I wanted to make sure I'd remember to ask him to sign it. I can't see how that can be insulting to you."

"Come off it, Anthea. You know in the first place, we will spend most of the evening talking about the book. And when did you forget anything you wanted to do in your life?"

Anthea gave a patient smile. "I can't see how this is any concern of yours. It's funny to know somebody as well as I know you and still not be able to follow the workings of his mind. It's my not being Irish, I suppose."

"It's your being an insensitive bitch," he replied.

Her face expressed nothing, but his could not conceal the shock he had given himself.

"I'm sorry," he said.

She looked as if she hadn't heard him and was making a

decision about some other matter on the distant horizon. He would not have been surprised if she had taken out a diary and made a note. Then she swallowed the end of her drink and looked at her watch.

"I had better see how the lamb is getting on in the oven."

"What have I done?" he asked himself, when he was alone. He had hit out in frustration; if she had hit back they would be closer now; not like this, cardboard characters in someone else's play.

"Shall I ring up?" she said when she came back. "They're half an hour late."

"Give them a little longer." He tried to put a conciliatory note into his voice.

"Like another drink?" he said. She was fussing over flowers in a vase. She had filled the place with flowers. It must have cost her a fortune.

"I think I'll wait, thank you. Give yourself one." The edge had gone off her voice too.

"You must think I'm very dim; but I'd be grateful if you'd explain what exactly you meant by what you said just now."

There was no hostility in this, as she said it; but a quite genuine puzzlement. They had never talked out any problem before, because they didn't ever have any problems. They walked on water or the seas divided and let them through.

"I don't know what you want me to explain," he said.

"You accused me of deliberately insulting you. I never did that or dreamt of doing it, unless you think it is an insult to you that I should buy Tony's book."

"*Tony.*"

"Yes. Tony. What else am I to call him? You weren't going to suggest that we Mistered and Missused one another all evening, were you?"

"It was only the way you said it."

"I don't know any other way of saying Tony."

"Forget it."

27

"We can't talk to each other if you are going to pick on everything I say. If you object to my calling Anthony Ward by his christian name I can see that you might object to my buying his book. One is not more unreasonable than the other."

"I said forget it. What I thought made you look silly was laying out his book like that. It is so amateurish. The sort of thing one of your blue-rinsed American dames would do."

"Thanks."

"We can't get anywhere if we are not honest with each other."

"Very well. I take it that the insult was my recognising any other writer except yourself."

"What a rotten thing to say."

"Let's close the subject. It is getting us nowhere."

She studied her nails. Her refusal to meet his note of intensity deflated him. What a misleading cliché that was about 'talking the same language'. If she was talking Chinese he couldn't feel more remote, and only three days ago they had been able to communicate with half a word. He felt desperate. Anything would be better than this coldness. She was freezing him out.

"Anthea," he said, "we can't be quarrelling when these people are here."

"That's up to you. I'm not quarrelling."

"You know very well what I mean. I don't want them to sense an atmosphere. One always does in someone else's house. I told you I was sorry for taking you up like that when you invited them. I did think you might have talked it over with me first. It's not as if they were old friends. You met the man for a moment at a crowded party and nothing would do you but to invite him to dinner. I wonder what his wife thought."

"I gave her the invitation. She seemed pleased. If she hadn't wanted them to come, she only had to refuse."

"Don't get me wrong. I've no objection to the Wards coming. Why should I have? And this is your flat, and you can ask anyone you like into it. I only thought that as it was our first entertainment, and they didn't happen to be friends of ours, you might have . . . Anyway, let's drop it. I've said over and over again that I'm sorry. What do you want me to do? Go down on my knees and beg?"

"You twist everything I say. I can't discuss anything with you. You've worn that martyred air ever since Monday. You keep on telling me you're sorry as if you wanted me to applaud you on the road to Calvary. You know very well that everything here is ours. If I hadn't felt that so firmly I wouldn't have invited the Wards. We've talked so often about the cosy little dinners we were going to give. They were so pleasant and friendly. You are both Irish authors. She is most attractive. I was flabbergasted when you went into a huff. I still can't understand it. And you know very well your spectacular forgiveness is quite hypocritical. You see yourself as hard done by."

"You are the hypocrite. You found him attractive and any author turns you on. All that business about his being of interest to me is sheer bull, and well you know it. I was born and brought up in Ireland. Ward has been there twice, staying in hotels. He is a pure cockney; and I object to his exploitation of this Fleet Street image of Ireland. I haven't looked at the book, and I don't intend to; but I gather from the notices that it is the standard formula—gunmen and their molls with the usual dosage of sex instruction for beginners thrown in."

"I think it is beautifully written."

"Oh, you have read it, have you?"

"He was coming to dinner after all . . ."

"I shall let him understand perfectly politely that I haven't read it. Only a beginner takes offence at not having been read by everyone."

"I still think it's pleasanter to have read his book before he comes."

"Anthea, why should we let people like the Wards come between us? What do they matter? We were perfectly happy before we met them. Now they seem to have taken over our lives. I beg of you . . ."

He moved towards her clumsily. She had been like this in the taxi coming home from the fatal party. A pillar of salt. Before that they had never been able to sit side by side without holding hands at least.

"Have you fallen for him. Is that it?"

She turned towards Brian slowly and looked at him with an impartial face. "I never thought anyone could be so riddled with jealousy."

"I am nothing of the kind. But I can't help thinking—"

"Thinking what?" A sudden sharpness had come into her voice. He felt threatened by it.

"Can't we forget the whole thing? Here, let me give you another drink. We shall die of thirst if we wait for the Wards. I suppose they will arrive before bedtime. I dare say they are doing a round of parties."

Anthea put a hand over her glass. "You have a remarkable way of avoiding questions. It enables you to say whatever you please, and then run for cover."

"Jesus! I only suggested that we forget about the Wards until they come. Then we can devote the evening to them."

"You asked me if I had fallen for Ward. Then you said that you couldn't help thinking. What I want to know, if you please, is what you couldn't help thinking."

"If you want to know, I'll tell you. When you met him at that party you went on like a schoolgirl."

"Well?"

"That's all."

"It's by no means all. It's only the beginning. I want to know what you couldn't help thinking."

"I told you, that you must have fallen for him."

"You know what you are saying?"

"I'm telling you what I saw with my own eyes."

She smiled patiently, as one talking to the afflicted. "Of course I was polite. The party was for them and on account of his book; and he was being pleasant and unaffected about it. What would the party have been like if everyone followed your example and went and sulked in a corner?"

"We've gone over that a thousand times."

"You were sulking because the party wasn't for you and the book wasn't yours. That strikes me as a pretty dog-in-the-manger attitude."

"Thank you."

"If you had thought about anyone else except yourself for half a moment you would have seen that most people were trying to help him to celebrate as they would have made you the centrepiece if it had been your party."

"That's all very well; but you should have seen your face when you came across the room to let me know he was coming to dinner. You are not going to tell me—"

"What precisely am I not going to tell you?"

"That you hadn't taken a fancy to him."

"I thought they were a more than usually attractive couple."

"I like the way you drag her in."

"Didn't you think she was attractive?"

"Why can't you be honest enough to admit that you were turned on by him?"

"Does this mean I am not to be civil to men I meet at parties? You were very anxious that I should try to impress your friends."

"I was proud of you. I wanted to show you off."

"I'm not to talk to anyone without first getting your approval, is that it?"

"You know very well what I mean. We go out and meet this fellow. You haven't said 'Hello' before you've invited him to a recherché little dinner in your recherché flat. It isn't so long since I met you and you invited me to a recherché little dinner—"

She was on top of him then hitting his face with her fists. He concentrated on holding her off without hurting her. He was perfectly cool-headed, and grateful that she had provided this distraction because he had gone too far.

They had congratulated themselves so often on the intuition that had brought them so effortlessly together; no hesitation; no looking back; no petty calculations. They knew at once. He endowed her with all his worldly goods when he moved in with a battered suitcase. "Everything is ours, ours," she said when he had been nervous about walking on her carpets. "I always know at once," she said, when he wondered at the way their lives had altered in an evening.

He had brooded over the phrase. He knew nothing about Anthea except what she told him.

She had stopped struggling now. He forced her head round and kissed her. She responded fiercely, and then started to struggle again. "That was a mean thing to say, about the meanest thing . . ."

"Forget it. When I saw you so moonstruck by that fellow, I got mad."

"That doesn't entitle you to call me a whore."

"When did I ever call you a whore?"

She pulled herself away from him and sat with her head down, looking plain.

"Anthea, for Christ's sake!"

"You aren't generous enough to value anything that is freely given. You must have the satisfaction of having had the better of the bargain or something that belonged to somebody else. You are typically Irish, if you will allow me to say so."

"Well, what did you mean when you said you *always knew*?"

"I don't know what you're talking about."

"That first night here, I asked you how you could be so certain about everything. We had only met once and talked for about ten minutes. You never hesitated."

"So that's what has been bugging you."

"It didn't bug me in the least until now."

"I can't believe that. You've been chewing on this a lot. I can hear it in your voice."

"It is only things you let slip, and all this excitement about a man you've met for the first time. Of course it has bugged me."

"Perhaps you have made a mistake. I accepted you as you were. I didn't ask to see your good conduct medal. I didn't pretend to be anything in particular. I thought you accepted me as I was."

"I thought we had fallen in love. I thought that excluded everyone else. If it doesn't mean that to you, then what am I doing here?"

"I didn't say I wanted anyone else."

It was now quite dark; the street lights had come on outside creating the effect of moonlight. He put out an indecisive hand when she rose, but she seemed unaware of his presence as she turned on lamps and pulled across curtains.

"We might as well begin," she said, sitting down at the table. He said nothing. "I can't see any point in your not eating," she said.

Her mouth was full of avocado pear. He sat down beside her.

"Go on," she said, pointing with her spoon. "Eat it."

The avocado, tricked out with some unfamiliar sauce, was good. He finished it and took another. "They won't be coming now," he said. He hadn't realised how desperately hungry he was.

There was one pear left. He passed it to her.

"Take it yourself. I don't want it."

He ate a third. "They are only halves," he said, rubbing the sauce off his chin.

She left the room and came back with the next course. "The lamb is ruined," she said.

He had seen a bottle of champagne in the refrigerator; until she decided to produce it, he confined himself to whiskey. He offered her some. She made no effort to stop him when he half-filled her tumbler. By taking more than usual she made him feel her need of comfort too. He had seen himself as the injured one. When she finished the whiskey, he gave her more without asking and drank some more himself. They forgot about the other courses and let the coffee preparations go for nothing.

The first to wake up in the morning, he lay very still, reassembling the fragmented evening in his mind before he turned round to look at Anthea's face upon the pillow.

She looked very young, very peaceful, and very far away.

How could he reconcile that child-face with the woman that he had quarrelled with so bitterly or the princess that had taken him into her palace or the woman moaning in his arms last night? He tried—his head was sore—to remember exactly how the evening ended. They had fallen out of the chair on to her Persian rug. He remembered pulling a cushion down. But what had happened after that?

Leaning on his elbow over her, he liked the image of himself protecting her. But he didn't want the day to begin. He didn't want to get back into the world. Even if they stayed in bed all day, letters would rattle in the box, the telephone would ring. Sometime or other they would have to get up and let life suck them in. Happy little clouds were scudding across a sky innocently blue. Would she come out on an excursion into the country somewhere? He would have liked to have arranged and managed the outing, but the car was hers; he wasn't qualified to drive it. Being driven by her would not be quite the same thing.

One of her eyes, wide open, was staring at him. He kissed it. He put his arms round her. He held her close. She knitted into him.

"What would you like to do?" he said.

"Now, you mean?"

"Later."

"I don't want to think about *later*."

Later, he had to get up anyway so he made coffee. Then the telephone rang. They had not switched it through to the bedroom.

"Let it ring," he said.

It rang and rang. They sat in silence as if a whisper would

betray them to the intruder. The ringing ceased. They still sat motionless for fear of starting it off again. Then the ringing began again.

"I'll answer it," she said, rolling out of bed. She had nothing on; and this plunged his mind back into the labyrinth of the evening, where it lost itself. She bent down, out of sight, and came up wrapping his shirt round her shoulders.

He knew at once from Anthea's tone that it was one of the Wards on the telephone explaining their failure to turn up; but he could not tell which. He sat up, straining his ears like a dog, to hear the voice at the other end of the wire.

When Anthea came back she had made more coffee and toast and set it out attractively on a tray.

"Do you want to see the paper, honey?" She had some letters which she hadn't opened.

"I hate the paper," he said. "It is full of monstrous irrelevancies."

She didn't answer. She was reading her letters. "Mmm," she said, folding them away. She didn't offer to say who they were from nor did she say which of the Wards had telephoned. He found that he couldn't ask her.

"Let me put marmalade on your toast," she said. For her there had been no interruption of the morning mood. Her hands were happy.

Then the telephone rang again. They listened; and they listened to each other listening.

"If we don't do anything, it will go away," she said. It did not.

"I'll answer it," he said. If the bell stopped now, he would spend all day wondering who it possibly could have been. . . .

"Hello," he said.

"Who was it?" she asked when he came back.

"I don't know. The phone cut off when I answered."

"He'd been ringing for ages."

"Why *he*?"

"Whoever it was."

"Nice of him to stop when I answered."

35

"It was probably a wrong number. Aren't you coming back to bed?"

"I might as well get up as I am up."

"That's an Irish bull."

"What's an Irish bull?"

"What you just said."

She lay back, smiling a sphinx smile. She was still lying like that when he looked in to see her before going out.

"Will you be in to lunch?" she asked.

"I'm not quite sure."

"Ring up when you know. I'll be here."

"I'll do that of course."

"Aren't you going to kiss me?"

He kissed her. The kiss told him nothing. She looked quite serene. She called after him affectionately.

In the street he discovered that his pockets were empty. From here, in Chelsea, it was a long way to anywhere he could pretend to have a reason to call. But he would not go back. It would be a first step in a retreat, and he was slowly mounting a new offensive. Why did she not say one of the Wards had telephoned? It would have been such an obvious and natural thing to do, calling for no comment from him. Not to mention it was deliberately evasive. Deliberately, because she knew he knew. It could of course have been simple prudence, not wishing to revive the controversy. She had certainly neither repeated the invitation nor accepted a retaliatory one. He had heard every word she said. But that second call? Did Ward ring back in the hope of finding her at home alone? It was very significant, that persistent ringing and then the abrupt hanging-up when he answered. It must have been Ward. Perhaps she was ringing him at this very moment.

The Tate settled the problem of filling in time. He walked listlessly from room to room—Constable, Turner, the pre-Raphaelites, the meaningless contemporary artifacts—none of them penetrated his soupy gloom. He had come here recently with her, when she raved over Tissot. Her true

period, she said. Tissot's girls had looked so gay that afternoon. They mocked his melancholy now. Those beauties in
their sea-breeze and garden freshness had been dead many
years. The Anthea that had smiled at them, *that* Anthea was
dead too. All so long ago. He went to the telephone; but he
had no money to make a call. He went to the desk where
postcards were on sale to look for a sympathetic face to
which he could explain his plight. But his nerve failed. He
pretended to choose cards, then put them back again. If he
walked quickly he would be home by half-past one.

Anthea looked pleased when he came in. "I would have
rung up," he explained, "but I found I had no money."

"It doesn't matter. You will have to put up with cheese
and biscuits. We can have the funeral meats for dinner."

He thought of several things to ask, to say, but rejected
each in turn.

"How did you manage if you hadn't any money?" she
said suddenly.

"Why do you ask that?"

"It only struck me this minute. If you had no money to
telephone, you couldn't have taken a bus."

"I didn't have to. I wanted to check a few details in the
Tate. I walked there."

"Details of what?"

"The Tissot pictures, as a matter of fact. I found myself
rather vague when I tried to write something about them."

"But we have the Tissot book here."

"It's not quite the same thing."

He intended to dismiss the subject; but her interest had
been aroused. She was a prey to enthusiasm.

"This is very exciting. When may I see it?"

"See what?"

"Whatever it is you are writing about Tissot. What a
secretive man you are! You know how I went on and on,
and yet you never said you were actually going to write
about him. I didn't know you wrote art criticism."

"Oh, this is nothing like that. I was only taking notes for

future use. What did you do? That's far more interesting."

"I just lay there missing you."

"Any explanation from our friends?"

"I don't quite . . ."

"Did the Wards apologise?"

"She rang up this morning. You were here."

"You never said who it was."

"Didn't I?"

"No. You went out to the telephone and came back and never said a word."

"I supposed you knew."

"Did the other person ring up again?"

"What other person?"

"Whoever else was ringing and cut off when I answered."

"No one rang up."

They sat silent over coffee. Anthea got through several cigarettes. She started to clear away dishes. He offered to help. "Don't bother," she said. "Mrs Atkins is coming this afternoon. She'll wash up."

To get money to go out he was going to have to ask Anthea to cash a cheque. It was a formality to which he had grown accustomed. She never lodged the cheques. But, just now, he couldn't. Nor could he go through another bleak charade of pretending to have somewhere to go. He had never opened the parcel of papers he moved in with—exercise books and loose leaves of foolscap upon which there was evidence of former literary miscarriages. He pulled it out now. It was curious to discover the beginnings of stories and plays which he had completely forgotten. They hadn't survived their short-lived inspirations. They might have been written by anyone. One feature they all had in common : the hero had nothing to do. The manuscript of his novel was in a special envelope. His only sustained effort : it failed in the sense that it was overlooked by reviewers and did not attract purchasers; but it served as a passport. *It was responsible for his being here.*

He said that to himself not with any sense of achievement

but as one might in a nightmare be on the stage before a great audience and unable to utter a syllable.

With an air of purpose he abandoned his manuscripts and went into the bedroom. Anthea was lying on the bed with a book in her hand. She looked up without putting it away. Her expression was neutral.

"I want to talk to you," he said.

"About what?"

"I was rude to you just now."

"I didn't notice it if you were."

"Not rude, perhaps; but you know what I mean. The truth of the matter is I was upset by the way you behaved about the telephone call."

"Oh, for God's sake! I had forgotten all about it. I told you: Mrs Ward—Tina, or whatever her name is—said she put us down for Wednesday *next* week in her diary. She was full of apologies. I said 'too bad', and did not offer her a replay. And that's it. Why do we have to go over and over everything like this?"

"I only wanted to explain why I got mad. Just put yourself in my place: what would you have thought if I had answered the telephone and come back and never said a word about it? Wouldn't it have struck you as suspicious?"

"Suspicious? You sound like a detective."

"Look here: we can't survive if we don't trust each other."

"Right."

"Well then, why did you act in that way?"

"Act! I'm not given to acting. You are the actor here. You heard every word I said on the telephone. I thought we had had enough on the subject, and I decided to kill it. Could we agree to do just that right now?"

"I never want to hear of them again."

"Right."

And peace descended again; but it was not quite the same. Anthea raised the question of work. If Brian hadn't a book on hand, shouldn't he try to exercise his talents on a newspaper? As for herself, she had only come to London on an exploratory mission. She hadn't intended to settle down permanently; but in view of their present arrangement she, too, would look for work.

She got it at once, on a women's magazine; he was not so fortunate.

He met her for lunch each day; she was excited about her job, looked quite ravishing, and couldn't stop talking. She refused to be depressed by Brian's delayed start. "You'll get something, honey." She left the flat each morning immediately after breakfast; Brian took his time, but was always at the restaurant when she arrived at one o'clock. After lunch he made calls. One morning, just as he was about to set off, Anthea rang up.

"I can't meet you today," she said. "I promised the editor I'd do a job for him. I'll only have time to snatch a sandwich. There's a salad in the fridge you can lay into. I'll see you this evening. Kiss. Kiss."

She rang off before he had had an opportunity to say anything. He looked at the receiver in his hand as if it had got there by a trick. He went into the bedroom, threw himself on the bed, and lit a cigarette.

At first his thoughts were vague. Anthea was so happy these days that she didn't seem to notice his depression. She came home full of gossip. She had been commissioned to write articles about American life. She would need Brian's help, she said, with these. Her cheerfulness sometimes got him down. It seemed insensitive in the circumstances. What sort of job did the editor want her to do that cut so drastically into lunchtime? The editor. She was forever talking about the editor. Brian didn't listen carefully; his own plight preempted his closest attention. He had no picture in his mind of Anthea's editor. The editor of a women's magazine was not likely to interest him. She had said he was quite young. He was the source of the gossip that she brought home. They must spend a great deal of time talking to each other.

The telephone rang, making Brian's heart jump. It had

the effect of a calculated interruption by someone listening to his thoughts. He went out slowly to answer it, being one who did not allow telephones to exert a mastery over him. When he picked up the receiver, the caller rang off.

He put it down and waited for the telephone to ring again. His mind was racing now. The coincidence was too obvious. Whoever it was, it was not Anthea's editor. He was in the office with her. It must be Ward. There hadn't been a word about him recently. Who found Anthea her job? She had not been very specific about the details; it had all been rolled up into a happy story which fitted in with her magic touch. She had got herself into a magazine with the same ease as she had taken Brian into her flat and into her bed. All the devils had come out again. He couldn't lie down any more. He must be up. He must be doing. Anthea's office was some-where in the Bloomsbury area; he wasn't quite sure where; he hadn't listened very carefully. He had her telephone number though. He had only to ring her up. The sound of her voice would restore his balance. He dialled the number. Anthea answered. He said, "Hello, is that you, Anthea?"

"What's the matter, honey?"

"I just wanted to say I might be a little late this evening. I'm meeting some people in El Vino's."

"That's all right, honey."

"Bye, then."

"Bye."

What good had that done him? Then he remembered that Anthea had been rather insistent that he should lunch at home, said something about a salad. Did she want him not to go to the restaurant? Was she going there with someone else? It was close to her office.

It was now one o'clock. He had to change trains to get to Holborn, the nearest station. With luck he would make it in three-quarters of an hour. But he had no luck; and it was two o'clock when he arrived at the restaurant. It was still crowded. 'Their' table was behind a pillar. He couldn't see it from the entrance, and had to push his way through the crowd.

Anthea was sitting with her back to him. There was nobody else at the table. Before he reached it, she stood up and met him face to face.

He stood gaping at her.

"Where have you come from?" she said.

He could find no words to say.

"I have to go back to the office."

"I know. May I come with you?"

"Of course."

They had to negotiate their separate ways through the throng. Outside Anthea said, "I didn't see you in the restaurant."

"I only came in just then."

"Then you haven't had anything to eat."

"That doesn't matter."

"I thought you were going to have something at home. You must get yourself a sandwich at least."

It was easier to agree to this. He had found her. She was alone. His behaviour looked odd enough without his going on hunger-strike.

"I'll go back and get some lunch before the place closes."

"I'll see you later. About when?" she said.

"The usual time."

"You said you were going to El Vino's."

"I've called that off. I'll be at home to greet you when you come back from the office."

She nodded; if she thought his manner strange, she hadn't let on. He looked after her. How graceful she was! But if she had hurried or looked back or done something to show she shared his agitation he would have felt less isolated and futile. For an instant he thought of following her. Not to let her go. And then he began to run in the opposite direction. He must get back to the restaurant and look at the table before it was cleared. By getting up when she did she had hidden it from view. Were there two coffee cups? And why had she not paid the bill?

When he got back a coloured waitress had just finished clearing the table.

"I beg your pardon," he said, "but were there two people sitting here just now?"

"No. The table is free."

"I know. But I was looking for a friend of mine. There was a lady here. Was there anyone with her?"

"I don't understand. The table is free. Can I get you anything?"

"A cup of coffee and a chicken sandwich."

When she returned he asked the same question very slowly, very clearly, very civilly. "You better speak to the manageress," the waitress said. Then she went to a customer at another table. She looked bored.

Brian ate and drank very slowly. He had all the afternoon to fill in.

PORN

―――――――――

"**W**E D O N ' T G E T weather like this very often," Daphne said to herself. "I think it's a shame Peter shuts himself up in the house."

She was lying on her stomach in the long grass at the end of the garden. Little by little she had shed her garments, and now she was wearing only a bra and briefs. If only Peter would put his book away and come and lie beside her and divest himself of some of his clerkly gear, it would be quite exciting. But she knew that there was not the least possibility of this happening, and that Peter would look at her now with disapproval. Some day she would get drunk, not necessarily on wine, but on the magic of the evening, as when she heard a man's voice in the valley yesterday singing on his way back from work, and then she could tear off all her clothes and go rushing through the fields, just once, to make up for all the time she had spent sitting upright in a chair, her knees together, while Peter read the newspaper—oh, so slowly—or made up his accounts. Sometimes he sat with her when he was reading, but he usually preferred—as today—to shut himself into his book room, where he couldn't be interrupted.

He had been on his way to the priesthood when he found that his true vocation was for the care of books. Daphne was working in the local library when he was appointed to take charge of it. She had nobody to love, and it pleased her to help him in all sorts of little ways; in the library first of all; but later her duties extended gradually until she found herself at last nursing him when he went down with a pernicious type of influenza.

44

A nun in the convent spoke to her about this, for her own good. Alarmed—or not so alarmed, perhaps, as it seemed to her at the time that she was—she told Peter exactly what the nun said. He got very worried about it. He had many dislikes and few enthusiasms; being the subject of gossip was what he disliked most of all. The matter grew out of all proportion, but only inside his own head, and when he sought advice from an old friend he had made up his mind that the only way to silence wagging tongues and secure domestic comfort was to marry the source of both. That was three years ago.

She lay so close to the earth, it seemed to move under her with the lazy motion of the sea on a hot summer day when it sighs and rises and sinks again as if the effort were too much. She pictured her husband at his desk, so thin and prim, the tips of his fingers together, his eyes buried in his book. Whenever she said she wanted something to read he insisted on trying to improve her mind. He had a great liking for Irish novelists of Victorian times—Kickham, Banim, Griffin—he said they were unfairly neglected and pressed them upon her and got annoyed when she showed a lack of enthusiasm.

"I'd like something with a bit of life in it," she said.

This he never attempted to supply, so she had to save from the housekeeping money to buy paperbacks. Books being the business of Peter's life, he found nothing amiss in spending large sums on buying them. But they were too learned by far for Daphne. He kept them locked up in his study. She was never allowed even to look at them.

From across the fields came the same voice that she had heard yesterday, a fine tenor voice singing a song that used to be very popular when she was a little girl. Who, she wondered, could it be? There was nobody she could think of that she could associate with so romantic a sound. She was overcome with a sudden longing, an ache inside her, an urge to break through the hedge and chase across the fields and throw herself into the arms of the singer. Perhaps he was at the haymaking. It would be very convenient, and more becoming in the sight of God surely than sitting in a closed room reading a dull book, flying in the face of nature, denying the light.

Wild thoughts. But Daphne was not a wild woman; she was a rather prudent one with—and why not?—natural longings. A cloud passed over the sun; a moment and it was again at full blaze, but the sudden cooling and darkening acted on Daphne like a warning. She was a girl who must be for ever doing things—a Martha not a Mary—and it was typical of her to wish to make up to her admirable husband for the wanton thoughts in which she had been indulging. If it were nothing else he might on this hot afternoon enjoy a cup of tea. She wanted also, but this she could not explain to herself, to try to share with him the quickening of her blood, her sense of unity with nature, so close today that she had felt the earth's pulse and heard its heart-beat. She took off all she had on, and put on in its place the light frock she had been wearing; then she went into the house.

Whenever she came into his room he looked up at once, and spoke in a rather impatient voice, half turning his head to do so. Why are you interrupting me? Please say what you have to say as quickly as you can and go away and leave me alone. All this was suggested by his meagre gesture and reluctant tone of voice. He seemed to resent any interruption and grudge every second of his time that was taken from his books.

Today Daphne refused to be intimidated. It was not complimentary to any wife to have it made so clear to her that she was of less importance than reading matter, but she put up with it, because she knew that he was a man of vast learning and she was very ignorant. She put up with it, but not today. When he refused a cup of tea, she said it was a shame to waste such a lovely day, why would he not take his book out of doors and read it somewhere in the shade.

"I can't read out of doors. I get distracted. Can't you leave me alone. Can't you see I'm perfectly happy as I am."

She looked at a man wrapped up like a brown-paper

parcel, sitting stiffly in a musty room. Through the window she could see nesting martins wheeling in the air; but he had placed himself so that he could not be distracted by the view out of the window.

"Come outside and enjoy the fresh air," she said. "It's lovely out there. The sun is shining."

Without encouragement, she crossed the threshold and advanced towards him with a light in her eyes that he had never seen before. He closed his book and pushed it out of reach under some papers as she put her arms round his neck and pressed his face against her large soft breasts. Their colour and form and texture were not a matter of conjecture. She was wearing nothing under her dress. She managed without any co-operation from him to settle herself on his knees. She opened a button on his shirt slowly, then another, then another.

"Well, blast whoever it is anyway!"

An imperious knock had sounded on the door. It was not to be denied. Wrapping her dress round her to clothe the area in which her husband had been so nearly suffocating, she went to see who the untimely caller might be.

The butcher's boy, with a parcel intended for another house, and without the loin chops Daphne had ordered. She could be pardoned if she spoke sharply, as she did.

Instead of going back at once to her husband she went to the kitchen and prepared a delicious tea for him. Not only the drink itself, made with little bags, but home-made bread, fresh butter, honey, and a sponge-cake on which she placed a fat dollop of cream.

Peter liked his food and had the sweet tooth of the non-smoker. Daphne did well to appear again with her cheerful tray, and if he put away his book with a martyred expression, he made short work of the meal. Daphne had placed the tray on a chair beside the large black sofa, upholstered in horse-hair, which was in that room because there was no other place in the house to put it.

When all that was left of the cake was the splodge of cream

which Daphne removed with a little handkerchief from Peter's petulant lips, he would have returned to his desk had she not held him down. What had come over her? She was not less surprised than he. Once more she put her arms round him; but this time she ran her lips all over his face with the action of an electric razor. At the same time she began to open his shirt, but not slowly now, impatiently, reckless when a button resisted. "You don't want this," she said, pulling off his coat; and the same it seemed went for his shirt which followed it on to the floor.

Disorder of any kind upset Peter; he cast a commiserating glance at the garments on the linoleum, but he was in no position to improve their situation. He was in a tidal wave which was carrying him out to sea. Any sense of decency and moderation that had ever possessed this girl he had married abandoned her now. He took off his trousers only because it seemed less shameful than to have them ripped off him.

"Shouldn't we go upstairs?" he said, clinging to the last spar of convention.

She didn't answer; she had the appearance of a frenzied seamstress with mouth full of pins, working against time. He had one thought only, to get it over. Only then could he get back to his book.

She wouldn't get up and go when he obliged her, as he did in his fashion. For a moment he had been at one with her; but it had passed. Now he wanted only to return to his occupation. She snuggled against him; she gently patted his cheeks, and gave little baby kisses to his bony ribs. Would she never be done?

And then the blessed butcher's boy rang at the door again. "Let him hang himself," she said. Poor boy who had no pleasure delivering meat in that weather. It was not to be. He must be attended to. And it was she who had to attend.

When she returned she found Peter dressed and sitting at his desk poring over the book he had not let her see when she embraced him. He was so absorbed in his studies he did not hear her come in, although her bare feet made a slapping

48

sound on the linoleum; nor did he look up when she whispered loudly.

"Sweetie, I'm back."

His mouth was very slightly open; twice while she watched him he wet his lips with a thoughtful twist of his tongue.

"Sweetie, I'm back."

Surely he must have seen her by this time. He moved a hand very slowly to turn a page as if he was trying not to lose what he was leaving.

"Sweetie, I'm—"

It was no use. She went back to the garden.

THE WIDOWS

T H E Y   H A D N ' T   H A D what anyone would call a conversation for upwards of twenty years and yet, since his
death, Mirabelle had been miserably lonely. She hadn't
been able to work up sufficient energy to cook for herself;
the garden, which she had brought to such near perfection,
was already tangled with weeds; plants, run to seed, gave it
a fantastic appearance. Even in the care of her own person,
she found herself pulling on the same clothes each morning;
and it seemed so much trouble to go through the preparations for a bath that more often than not she satisfied herself
with a lick and a promise.

For a few days after the funeral neighbours dropped in,
doing little acts of kindness and offering her hospitality; but
she had been so wan in her responses that their good resolu-
tions soon fell into decay. It was not a betrayal of any kind,
when Ernest was alive the Millets kept to themselves; the
extent of their social life was a short interchange of civilities
when they met acquaintances in the street. Not that anyone
had seen Ernest out of doors for years; he spent most of his
time in his bedroom, just pottering about, to emerge at the
moment when he was least expected demanding a meal.
Mirabelle's ingenuity was taxed by this unreasonable habit;
but it was useless to expect Ernest to change now. He had
always been eccentric, but kind in essentials. He was the sort
of person who accepts nothing he reads or is told without
examining it first. As conversations with her husband always
entailed an argument, Mirabelle, who found difficulty in
putting sentences in proper order, avoided them. With anyone else who was friendly enough to listen, she would go

rambling on for hours; but a short answer to a clear question was as far as she went with her husband; and as they slept in different rooms nowadays, they were living to all appearances like perfect strangers.

Mirabelle sometimes sighed for company; but visitors were few because Ernest came downstairs if there were a caller, and stood watching until the door closed behind them, or sat in silence in a corner if Mirabelle's offer to take a chair was accepted by the visitor. This carry-on made people nervous.

There was nothing nervous about Susan, the Millets' only daughter. Her raids were regular; and it took the rest of the day for the dust to settle after she made her flying departure to get home in time to have tea ready for her husband, Fred Taylor, a bank manager in Bray. "How's Pop?" she said first thing when she arrived and was taking her coat off and casting an eye round to see if there had been a change made in anything since her last visit. Ernest did not come down when he heard Susan's arrival. It told him all he wanted to know; and she sometimes went home without having seen him.

Mirabelle liked to show Susan what she had been doing in the garden; it was discouraging to go to so much trouble and to be the only person to appreciate it: Ernest hadn't been in the garden since the time the fox got into the hen-house. (Mirabelle had screamed and screamed.)

Ernest died in exactly the manner you would have expected. Mirabelle, feeling unaccountably nervous, took a long time to get to sleep on the night of Hallowe'en. It may have had something to do with the barmbrack. When at last she dropped off, Ernest came into her room and stood beside the bed until she woke up. She gave a cry of fright. "I thought for a moment you were a man," she said. Since Ernest was always the one to speak first she waited, and only when she thought that he must be feeling cold, standing there in his pyjamas without a dressing-gown on him, she said, "Is anything the matter, Ernest?"

"I have a pain."

When she asked him where he had the pain, he said the question was irrelevant as she was incapable of ministering to any pain anywhere, not having been trained in medical science.

She enquired if the pain were bad, and he said that if it were not he would hardly have woken her up in the small hours. When she said she would ring up Doctor Crossley, Ernest said—which was true enough—that the doctor wouldn't be grateful to her for waking him up at three o'clock in the morning. They were clearly in an impasse; that wouldn't have bothered Mirabelle in the ordinary course, efforts to talk about things with Ernest always ended up like this, but she was worried about the pain because Ernest had never had one before; and if Ernest had a pain it would not be like anyone else's. Instead of starting another argument, Mirabelle took up the telephone and dialled Doctor Crossley's number.

"Ernest has a pain," she said to the sleepy voice that answered the telephone. The doctor—as Ernest had foretold did not sound pleased to hear about it. She put her hand over the mouthpiece and whispered very loud, "He wants to know where the pain is?"

"Inside," Ernest said.

"He says it is inside," Mirabelle repeated. There was a confused sound at the other end of the wire. "Doctor Crossley will come round in the morning first thing," Mirabelle said, putting down the telephone.

"I'll be dead," Ernest said. And he was.

"Your father never liked a fuss," Mirabelle told her daughter when she called to see if she could help in any way. Left to herself, Mirabelle would have dug a hole in the garden and put Ernest comfortably in, as she put the dogs and cats that she had loved through the years when they died. It was very sweet and peaceful in the garden, except the night the fox came.

Mrs Taylor went home and told her husband that they

would have to do something because her mother was quite helpless. Then Mr Taylor rang up the undertaker and the solicitor and the newspapers and the clergyman—in that order.

Mirabelle behaved in a vague and unsatisfactory way at the funeral. She insisted on wearing a hat she had made herself for the occasion, it was of yellow straw and had a ribbon which tied under her chin.

"Mother! You can't wear that, you look like a gipsy." But Mirabelle, who gave in to everything her daughter said as a rule, stood her ground. Her hat had nothing to do with anyone but herself, was how she saw it. But if she got her way in the end, it ruined the funeral. Susan was cross because she knew her husband hated more than anything being made to look foolish. He kept Susan close beside him as if he wanted to make it quite clear that this was the woman he was married to. Mirabelle stood apart, by herself, and wondered if Ernest knew what was going on.

Afterwards, with the solicitor, Mr Taylor was able to show himself at his best. He was so practical, so long-headed. Ernest had never told his son-in-law about his business. And he was unable to conceal his curiosity from the experienced lawyer, or his satisfaction when he heard that Ernest owned some house property. "Your mother is provided for," he was able to tell Susan. To the solicitor, he said, "See that she makes a will."

Mirabelle showed no interest at all in her financial position. So long as she didn't have to move out of the house and garden, nothing else mattered very much. She could cook and sew and garden and look after herself and live on very little, she said. There was no reason why life should change. The only difference Ernest's going made in practice was that she now hadn't to wonder when he would appear and ask for a meal.

She was able to plan her day in advance but, for some reason, she couldn't bring herself to do anything except feed the animals and clean out the budgerigar's cage. Her thoughts were all about the past; she found she was asking herself questions about things that happened long ago and couldn't be answered now. Everyone else was dead. She had a picture in her mind of her father whom she knew only through her mother's description. It had satisfied her until now; but there was so much else to know about him that she had never found out; and now it was too late. Above all, she wished someone had told her what was in Ernest's mind when he married her.

Because she was inclined to do what she was told by anyone—except in little things like the hat for the funeral—when Ernest asked her to marry him she accepted at once in her mind, but all she had been able to say was, "We had better wait until September; we always go to the seaside in August."

The arrangements were made between Ernest and her mother, who were nearer contemporaries. It was a very quiet wedding because the Millets had no relations they were in touch with. Ernest had a brother who acted as best man. Two of the neighbours came. After the wedding there was a modest entertainment at Mirabelle's mother's house. Nobody seemed to have anything to say; and it was a relief when Ernest saw the taxi at the gate and said there was no sense in allowing it to run up a bill for waiting.

The honeymoon was spent in the Strand Palace Hotel in London. Mirabelle had never been away from home before, except to go to the seaside. The crowds in London seemed to threaten her—so many strange faces—the noise, the rush and whirl of the traffic. What pleased her best was a flower-seller's stall close to the hotel entrance. She could hardly drag herself away from it, and stood staring at the flowers until Ernest became impatient. She was a little bit scared by Ernest; but she felt safe with him. She was curious about what was going to happen when they went upstairs; and when Ernest took a very long time over the dinner in the hotel—he ate very deliberately and slowly—she longed to say, "Hurry up." Not because she was looking forward to anything or wanted to get it over; but it was the way she always was when she had to wait for anything to begin.

When they did go up to their room, she undressed very quickly, was in her nightie and tucked up in the bed before Ernest had unpacked his suitcase. She didn't wash her face or brush her teeth or fold her clothes. Ernest performed all these operations with the deliberateness with which he did everything; but then, he had been doing them for twice as long as Mirabelle had been alive. She could only hear him, because she kept her head deep in the pillow and the bed-clothes up round her ears. But she recognised every sound, and even began to anticipate them as, for instance, when he was brushing his teeth; she timed almost to the precise moment when he would spit into the basin. She had heard each garment come off, and he gave a little groan before his shoes dropped, thud, thud, on the floor.

Then he turned the light out.

She knew in general outline what she and Ernest had to do although she had no idea how he would go about it. She was not frightened, but she was curious. It would have been easier if they had been friendlier, but she hardly knew Ernest, and he said so very little. He was working for the Gas Company when she met him; her mother was having constant worry with the supply—they lived rather off the beaten track—and Ernest had come out from town to see what the matter was.

Mirabelle's mother, who was kind to strangers, offered him a cup of tea. While he was drinking it, he stared at Mirabelle, who didn't mind, because she was sewing a dress she was making and she thought he was interested in watching her at work. She always watched people at work herself, and learned a great many of the things she knew in this way —how to make butter for instance, how to drive a tractor, how calves and little pigs are born.

She was surprised and grateful when Ernest put his arms round her and hugged her. It was comfortable and warm, and not at all as she had imagined he would behave. She had expected him to give her directions like the men on the farm did when she offered to help them at whatever they were doing. She had taken it for granted that she would get on perfectly well with Ernest whatever his manner of proceeding; she always got on with people because she was eager to help and willing to learn. Talking was the trouble; and Ernest talked even less at night than by day.

When he seemed to need help at what he was trying to do, she gave it to him. She hadn't expected pain; but she knew it wasn't any fault of his unless, perhaps, he was in too much of a hurry.

She lay awake after he fell asleep, looking at the ceiling upon which the moonlight made a pattern of white circles. It was an odd feeling to be in bed in a strange room with someone you hardly knew. Ernest was snoring contentedly as if he were playing trains in his sleep.

He had seemed old when she first saw him, and he had never grown much older, except in almost imperceptible ways. More wrinkles came; but they were as fine as cobwebs.

Susan made her appearance nine months, almost to a day, after the first night in the Strand Palace Hotel; and became at once the centre of Mirabelle's universe. Every kind of domestic animal was to be found in or around the Millets' house. Susan was the pick of the bunch, so long as she was a tiny thing. It was very clear very soon that she took after her father. She was very deliberate in all she did and did only one thing at a time; she was jealous of her possessions; she locked things away and then took them out and counted them, and shrieked if anyone went near them. She did not like to be touched.

Mirabelle tried to teach her lessons; but it was quite hopeless. She had never been able to explain what was in her head to other people. The child had to go to Ernest in the evening with her copybooks. He made it all so plain in so few words that Mirabelle felt ashamed in front of Susan who had watched her struggling so hard earlier in the day.

Ernest never interfered in Mirabelle's domain. She cooked

and washed and polished and sewed and kept the garden as
well as the hens, the ducks, the rabbits, the pigeons, the cats,
the dogs, the hedgehog, and whatever strayed or stricken
creature she happened to have taken in or was trying to
mend; but in the matter of Susan's education, when he saw
how lamentably the home lessons were going, Ernest called
on the nuns and arranged for her to be taken for lessons at
the convent, although she was much younger than any of
the other children in their little school.

Before she was in jeans, Susan was an old woman; at
school she bossed the children and, in due course, the nuns;
at home she took command. Mirabelle lived in awe of her,
and sought more and more the company of the pets, which
increased in number as Susan grew in efficiency. But nobody complained. It was a well-organised household with
each member employed in a separate compartment. Ernest,
now on pension, took no part at all in domestic or garden
chores. He cleaned his own room and disliked anyone's
going into it, paid the bills, and gave Mirabelle money every
week, telling her to spend it. She worked out over the years
an elaborate system of deceiving him, because she found his
allocation unsympathetic. He never saw through her little
fraud; but Susan did.

There was a tacit conspiracy between Susan and Ernest
for the management of Mirabelle. It encouraged her in her
whims and took advantage of her accomplishments. Susan
had no ambition to do the sort of work at which her mother
excelled. Anything that could be done by sight and touch
came naturally to Mirabelle. Susan did best whatever could
be learned out of a book. You could tell at a glance when
Susan arranged the flowers; they looked uncomfortable; when
Mirabelle put them in a vase they arranged themselves.

Ernest had been a Presbyterian in his youth, but never
attended any church; Mirabelle's religion like everything else
about her was vague. Why Susan was brought up a Catholic
was because the convent was so near. When Susan was being
confirmed—she liked a ceremony of any sort, provided she

57

was taking part—Ernest and Mirabelle were invited by the nuns to come and watch. Mirabelle never thought to disobey, but she was astonished when Ernest came downstairs in his wedding suit, having decided to come. Nobody said anything; but Mirabelle was wonderfully proud to be seen with him—"This is Ernest," she said to everyone—and Susan's cup of happiness overflowed. "She looks very plain, God love her," Mirabelle said to herself, but not to Ernest, who wouldn't have liked it.

Plain or not, it was somehow inevitable that Susan would marry whenever she made up her mind. She met Mr Taylor when she became a clerk in the bank at seventeen, with top place at entrance. Mr Taylor was looking for a sensible girl, and he found one in Susan. They married after four years' courtship.

Mirabelle missed her. She missed being bossed by Susan. She missed the strength Susan gave her, so that she didn't have to look to Ernest for support. Having that meal ready on time became the only link she had with him. But it was a compelling one. There was drama every day.

Susan had been married for three years when Ernest died. A month or so after the funeral, when Mirabelle was sitting at the fire with a cat on her lap, wondering how long the world would last, there was a knock on the door.

She began to think at once of all the people she hoped it wouldn't be, and this prevented her from opening the door although she had jumped to her feet with a guilty feeling when she heard the knock (the feeling she used to have when Ernest came downstairs hungry). A second rather dispirited knock, as if whoever it was hadn't expected to find anyone at home, followed. It quietened Mirabelle's fears. She opened the door.

A tinker woman who had come begging several times earlier in the year was standing very close to it. She looked woebegone.

Without waiting for Mirabelle to say anything she broke into a long litany, punctuated by tears. "Himself is after dying," was only part of all she said in such a rapid flow that Mirabelle could never have kept up with it at any time. But she knew how it would end, and she was asking herself where she had put her bag. It had a way of getting lost. Then she remembered it was beside the bread bin. She invited the tinker woman into the kitchen, and opened the bag. Three notes and some silver and copper lay inside.

"If you could spare me a shilling or two, I haven't the price of burying him," the visitor said, looking at everything except the bag. Mirabelle stared at the three crisp notes, and wondered what Ernest would say if he knew she was thinking of giving a five pound one away. But the woman was poor, and she, too, had lost her man. It was because of Ernest Mirabelle parted with the fiver.

"May God and his Holy Mother bless you," the woman said; but her eyes were covetous if her voice was grateful.

"Could you ever make it up to seven? I wouldn't ask if it wasn't for the childer."

Mirabelle had impressed herself by doing what neither Susan, much less Ernest, would have permitted, and she was disappointed to find that it hadn't made a similar impression on her visitor. She made good the default at once but without such a kind feeling this time. She didn't listen to the praises that were lavished on her; she wanted the woman to go away. But she lingered, babbling, darting sharp eyes into every corner of the kitchen.

"Could you ever," she said suddenly—as if the idea had only just occurred to her—"could you ever let me have a sup of whiskey for me mother. She's nearly dying herself of a cold she caught out in the storm last week. She was drownded in it. And there's nothing that would put the breath of life into her like a small sup of whiskey. I hate to ask you for it when you've been so good . . ."

Her speech slowed and her eyes followed Mirabelle when she went to a cupboard and took out an empty lemonade bottle. She filled this from the bottle of whiskey which she kept for emergencies. Emergencies included a severe head cold, a bad wetting, toothache, and an unexpected caller.

"Oh, that will put the power of life into her. Ah, you're very good, but you'll get your reward for it. Is that a lemonade bottle, you wouldn't by any chance have any with a drop of lemonade in, then? The childer was begging me to bring them back some, but since I haven't even the price of a shroud for their father . . ."

There was a cardboard carton with six bottles of lemonade in it on the dresser. Mirabelle handed it over.

"What will the childer say when they see what you've given them? They'll pray for you. I hate to ask you, when you're after doing so much for me, but would you ever have a bit of a rug or an old blanket that you could spare? If you were to see what the childer has to cover them at night . . ."

Ernest had an army blanket, acquired in a disposal sale after one of the world wars, which he kept in reserve for nights that were particularly cold. Mirabelle remembered exactly where it lay folded. Mesmerised, she went upstairs; but it wasn't on the shelf where she had seen it last. This gave her a shock; Ernest never moved anything. She opened the drawers of his cupboards, how neatly everything was put away! But there was no sign of a rug. When she had looked everywhere else, she glanced at the bed. There it was. Ernest had been using the rug on the night he died. Mirabelle didn't like taking the rug off the bed—she hadn't been in the room since Ernest left it—but she couldn't disappoint the widow after raising her hopes. Before leaving the room she prayed—to Ernest really—that the rug would be the last of these demands because—if only the woman knew —she was powerless to refuse her.

There were some issues—the hat at the funeral for example —upon which Mirabelle could not be moved; she was solid rock, but if anyone wanted something—they didn't even have to ask, she recognised the symptoms—she couldn't be at peace with herself until she gave it, whatever it was. And nowadays she felt attached to nothing. She had no use for the rug; but she wouldn't have agreed to give it had she known that it was on Ernest's bed. She felt as guilty as if she had stolen it from him.

The kitchen was empty. Mirabelle felt a sudden lightening of her heart, but only for long enough to take a deep breath; then she saw the visitor standing in the hall, with her nose turned towards the door, like a dog waiting to be let out. She took the rug without ceremony and with a brief "God bless you". Mirabelle regretted more than ever having robbed Ernest's room. But it was such a relief to see the tinker woman hurrying down the path that she decided it was worth it to get her out of the house.

She had no regrets about the money although it was all she had until the end of the week (Mr Taylor had made the arrangements). But the visit to Ernest's room—and what she did there—gave a focus to her sadness. "I have been feeling very low since Ernest died"—that is how she had described the state of her case to anyone she talked to, but now she realised that she was actually missing him. She was lonely. She had to love something. In any other person's life it would have been a coincidence that the hedgehog came in from the garden just then. Mirabelle picked it up in a way she had and nursed it in her lap.

Next day, the sun was shining brightly when Mirabelle came down to breakfast. On mornings like this the copper pot on the dresser came into its own and reflected its borrowed glory on the white wall of the kitchen. There was no copper pot on the dresser this morning. The pot was the only present Ernest had ever given her. Anything else he bought her, such as the dress she got married in, served some necessary purpose. He had seen the pot on a slag heap, and put a lot of work into taking the dents out of it without succeeding quite in bringing it back to its pristine shape. The lid was one Ernest had (he kept things), and it very nearly fitted. Mirabelle was charmed with the gift at the time and polished it. Mirabelle remembered the tinker woman in the hall, so eager to leave all of a sudden, when a moment before she had apparently established herself as a fixture. Her manner had changed while Mirabelle was upstairs; she was like someone who has seen an ugly-looking cloud in the sky and is hurrying to get home before the shower. The tinker woman must have stolen it.

Mirabelle pulled on an old coat of Ernest's, the first that came to hand when she opened the door of the closet. Out of doors, she turned right and walked towards the village. She walked resolutely, like a soldier, looking straight in front of her. There was no expression on her set face. When she reached the bridge, she turned off the road and took the path down to the river bank. There was a large expanse of waste-ground there; it had always been a favourite camping site for tinkers.

A sturdy man of about Mirabelle's age was leaning against a dilapidated caravan, reading a newspaper. Two aged horses were snuffling patiently over the places where there had once been grass. There was nobody else to be seen.

Mirabelle walked up to the man, who was watching her approach over the top of the newspaper. He waited for Mirabelle to speak.

"I've come for the copper pot," she said.

He looked round him as if in obedience to her whim, indulging her. At last he said good-humouredly,

"There's no copper pot here, miss."

"I won't go back without my copper pot."

"But I haven't got your copper pot. There isn't a copper pot in the place. What would I be doing with a copper pot? There's no tinkers nowadays."

A face peered round the back of the caravan, and then quickly withdrew. But not quickly enough. Mirabelle turned away from the man. He didn't try to prevent her when he saw where she was going.

"You can ask herself," he said.

The tinker woman was waiting for Mirabelle behind the caravan.

"I've come for the copper pot," she said.

"I haven't got your copper pot, woman dear. If I had you'd be welcome to it."

Mirabelle pushed past her and stared into the dark recess. On piled-up mattresses a bed had been made; the sheets were new and clean. She hadn't made a picture of what she was going to encounter. This was a home.

"Can't you listen to me, ma'am. There's no copper pot in it. I couldn't tell you a lie."

"I'm going to tell the Guards about the copper pot," Mirabelle said. The idea occurred to her only at that moment.

"Don't go near them fellows. You are a kind woman; you wouldn't have a day's luck after."

Mirabelle didn't hear. When set on something, she never did. She walked away as resolutely as she came. The man was not on view, but she saw Ernest's army rug lying with others of various kinds under a bush.

When she was at the bridge, she heard footsteps behind her; she didn't look round. She knew the woman was there.

"I'll bring you back your pot tonight," she panted. She had been running.

Mirabelle stood and faced her. "I want it now."

"But I can't give it to you now, alannah, because I haven't got it. I'll have to go and fetch it from the woman who has it; and I'll bring it down to your place then. I didn't want my brother to hear me. I wouldn't like him to know about anything like that. I'll be with you before seven."

"I'll wait till then."

"And you won't be talking to the Guards?"

"Not if I get my copper pot back."

On the way home Mirabelle met Mrs O'Higgins, one of her neighbours. She told her all about the copper pot. She would tell everyone she knew about the copper pot for years to come, but not Susan because she wouldn't approve of the way the story began.

Mrs O'Higgins listened kindly, mentally cancelling a visit to the church to pray for her youngest son's success in the leaving-certificate exam that day. When Mirabelle finished,

Mrs O'Higgins laughed. "So her husband's dead again, is he?" she said. Mirabelle enjoyed the joke too; but it made her anxious again. She had really believed the tinker woman. Now Mirabelle suspected that she had been made a fool of. But what could she do? She had promised not to report the theft to the Guards. She must give the woman until seven o'clock to perform her promise.

She came when Mirabelle was having her tea (boiled egg, two Ryvita biscuits, and a cup of Bovril) and thrust the pot, looking none the worse for its travels, into Mirabelle's hands. She was not wearing her black shawl; her red, man's shirt, open at the neck, revealed an expanse of satin-white skin which had nothing to do with the freckled and wind-tanned face. She had the clean smell of a fresh-washed cabbage.

Mirabelle could say nothing. She fondled the copper pot; the tinker woman watched her, looking as pleased and proud as if she had just restored a lost child to its mother.

They might have stood there indefinitely so far as Mirabelle was concerned, but the tinker woman after a little while said, "I'll leave it with you now. I told himself I was only going up the road for a minnit." And as Mirabelle walked back to the gate with her she looked up at her, smiling.

"Isn't the drink a divil?" she said.

When Mr Taylor had to go to London on business Susan came down—as she described it—to look after her mother. Mirabelle was delighted at first but—never at ease with her daughter—became increasingly apprehensive as the day drew near. Susan had such a genius for putting her in the wrong; and she was for ever talking about the price of things. Mirabelle swore her neighbours to secrecy about her alms-giving and its exciting consequences.

On the pretext that she had shopping to do, but really to escape from Susan for an irresponsible hour, Mirabelle went up to town on the second day of the visit, and spent the afternoon in a cinema. Feeling guilty but also triumphant she returned, expecting to be cross-examined, with a convincing story ready : she had forgotten it was early-closing day. However, Susan was too full of her own achievements to concern herself with her mother's; she had skimped the supper and solved that day's crossword puzzle. It was when they were eating the skimped supper that she remembered an afternoon incident—a woman had called begging for money and clothes; she had sung a familiar tune to the effect that 'the mistress' always obliged in these matters. Susan had been a match for her.

"I wasn't going to listen to any of that sort of nonsense, but she looked so woebegone that I took pity on her. She had been eyeing it from the moment she set foot in the kitchen—I gave her the old copper pot on the dresser. There's a hole in the bottom of it. I could never understand why you bothered to keep it."

BROTH OF A BOY

<hr />

"DREAMING AGAIN, JOHNNY," said his mother, running a worn hand over his uncombed hair. Johnny did not hear her; ever since earlier in the day he saw his former school-friend, Matt Grimes, stepping out of a Fiat four-door, his mind had been occupied with an absorbing problem. He had been unable to concentrate on any other subject and would so remain until he had thought the matter through to a conclusion. It was ironical that little Grimes of all people should have been chosen by Providence to disturb what had seemed since the previous evening to be a settled plan, but he might also have been sent to warn Johnny before it was too late. At least he had the opportunity to decide what exactly it was he wanted to do. Had he not seen Grimes and gone ahead with the other plan and discovered afterwards that he had made a mistake, his life might have been in a shambles.

"Shouldn't you be getting back to your work?" his mother said when she came in again and started to clear the table. She could not be still, but must forever be fussing round, and treated Johnny as if he were still a boy at school. He had been working for nearly two years now, and if contributing nothing to the running of his home, called on her for assistance only in times of crisis. He smiled wryly at the disparity between his preoccupation and his mother's estimate. He could afford to pity her; she would learn soon enough.

Last night, at or around midnight, Johnny Connolly decided to marry Lily Harrington. He was in close proximity to her at the time, but he did not disclose his intention. Her consent was a foregone conclusion. She had made that abundantly clear. Had there been an element of conflict at any stage he might have resolved it and in the flush of victory committed himself; but Lily had been a push-over from the start. Her admiration for Johnny was unmasked by guile, and he had been too complacent about it. Had Lily been less attractive her lack of finesse might have justified his casual acceptance of her devotion; but she was the prettiest of all his friends and the most elegant. 'A lovely dresser,' as he described her. The duplicity of Rosemary Harris, who had rather hairy legs, opened Johnny's eyes to the bargain he had been getting in Lily. Only just in time. Last night's proceedings would have reassured him—if reassurance were required —that Lily was unchanged. Where would he find a girl to match her? He had always had this idea that he would marry when he was twenty-one. An element of fatalism in his nature, perhaps. And if he were to bring it about, how fortunate to have Lily available. Were he to postpone the decision until he was earning more and had some prospect of accommodation, it was too much to hope that Lily would wait. She had a queue of admirers, and not all of them negligible by any means. Lily worked in the packaging end of the business. Johnny was in accounts.

Having arrived at his decision and slept on it, Johnny arose unshaken. His plan of action was simple and straightforward. He was seeing her home after the cinema; he would get Lily to name the day and give his mother the good news at breakfast when Aunt Julia was there. Aunt Julia was a dim-witted pensioner who helped Johnny's mother to pay the rent of their flat; she acted as a very useful breakwater; whenever Johnny had news to tell which his mother might not take to kindly, he made sure that Aunt Julia was in the audience. She could be counted on to support him and repeat his arguments (which sometimes conflicted) as if they were her own.

Having gone so far nothing would shake Johnny's resolution. Practical difficulties could always be overcome by ignoring them. With Lily beside him the wedding preparations would be pressed on. The wedding was what it was all about, he would say, scorning any obstacles that might be raised by the timid. There was something wrong with our society if it could not provide him and Lily with the wherewithal to marry. How long would it be before the people woke up to the absurdity of the banking system? Once Johnny decided to marry Lily, what had seemed a debatable proposition became an assertion of one of the rights of man. If Johnny were to be thwarted in this natural inclination his name would only be one more added to the roll of martyrs for social justice. He felt ennobled by the thought; but he had no intention of becoming any sort of martyr. Who could prevent him from marrying Lily when both of them had decided upon it?

This was the state of his mind when he set out from home for his office—a little late admittedly, but he had been out rather longer than usual with Lily the night before. The rush-hour was over; he had to wait an interminable time for a bus, but nothing could fray his temper this morning. Or so he thought until he saw Matt Grimes. The bus had stopped at a halt, giving Johnny time to see a car pull up on the side of the road, Matt emerge therefrom, stroll nonchalantly over to a letterbox, post some mail, return to the car, and engage the gears. At that moment the bus lurched forward, leaving Johnny in an advanced condition of nervous excitement. He never thought about Matt these days. He was one of those boys who don't seem entitled to an identity out of school, a natural extra in the film show of life. What was he doing with a motor car? There was always the possibility that it belonged to somebody else; but Johnny couldn't solace himself with the possibility. There was something distinctly proprietary in Matt's manner, a casual assurance, almost impossible to define. Put it this way : had the car been a girl, Johnny would have known Matt was married to her.

Cudgelling his brains, Johnny seemed to recall some other old school-fellow mentioning that Matt had started to work for a relation in the turf accountancy business. He had not been sufficiently interested to enquire further into the matter.

Whatever happened to himself in life, Johnny thought it a safe bet that Matt would always be out of sight somewhere in the dusty rear. In a bookmaker's office there would be no doubt duties humble enough to match his pretensions; it would never have occurred to anyone, surely, to let Matt get anywhere near the inflow of losing bets. But there was palpable evidence to the contrary; Matt was running a car.

Before Johnny arrived at the office, his brain was in a ferment; he looked inside every car that passed, and whenever he saw a young face behind the wheel he endured a promethean agony in his bowels. The pages of figures that opened before him on his desk became a meaningless mass of restless molecules. He was as unconscious of the head bookkeeper's sarcastic grimaces at the clock as of his neighbour's efforts to interest him in a verbal replay of last Saturday's football game.

Matt Grimes with a motor car! It was a condemnation of Johnny's mode of life. It was also a challenge.

When his mother rubbed her hand through his hair after midday dinner, she was innocently disturbing him at a moment when he was trying to resolve the greatest crisis of his life. Had he been able to bring himself to confide in her she would have tried to relieve his tension by urging that there was no time limit. He was under no compulsion whatever to reach an immediate decision. This showed how little his mother understood her son. Once he had decided upon anything, it must be done at once. Otherwise it might never be done at all. Having decided to get engaged that evening, the matter was settled so far as Johnny was concerned. Nobody could persuade him to agree to a postponement.

But this morning's apparition had undermined Johnny's resolution. The question he was asking himself was : should he drop the idea of the wedding and buy himself a car instead? It could be adduced as proof of his moderation that he never entertained for a moment the idea of doing both. He saw himself as confronted with an anxious choice.

The arguments for marrying Lily had all been considered. They were obvious. The hazards it had never occurred to him for a moment to consider. But now that he was forced to consider so serious an alternative, it was impossible to hold back the objections that might be raised by a disinterested adviser to the marriage prospect. Chief among them that it made the day when he could afford a car recede beyond the horizon. With a car of his own, his social life would expand. Not only would it raise his prestige among the group he was in, it would enable him to move into others. The picture of himself and Lily, huddled together in doorways, gave way to one in the comfortable womb of the car, at midnight on the top of a mountain or parked in a row with others, listening to the whisper of the sea. And in that picture he was a transformed being. His clothes were way out. His pockets were full of precious possessions, wallets, gold pencils, fountain pens. The handkerchief that had urgently to be pressed into use was pure silk.

Then the devil's advocate got to work. He told Johnny that the car would lead him ever further into debt. It would set him a standard to live up to, which would be wildly beyond his means. With Lily there would be a motive for economy. Whatever money there was would be required for the marriage. There would be no temptation to spend it on high living. This sobering thought robbed the idea of the marriage of its magic. Some of the married men in the office were little better than slaves.

There was this to be said, if anything went wrong with the car it could be got rid of. But once married ... He was ashamed. Although it was now after the official lunch hour, Johnny purged himself of that unworthiness by letting his mind play with a nobler prospect: he pictured a time when he could afford to be married and to have a car and to have a house. He saw himself sitting with Lily on either side of a blazing electric fire in a room in which the gaily-patterned carpet spread from wall to wall and the television-cum-radio-cum-stereo operated on all three levels at once.

He arrived back at work without having reached a decision. But he had the afternoon to think it over. He wasn't
meeting Lily until seven o'clock. For economy's sake, the
lovers ate at home on working days. So long as he had his
mind made up before they left the cinema it would be time
enough. Lily was inclined to be suspicious whenever he was
silent. "I love you," she'd keep on saying as if she was pulling
at the choke of a car that was refusing to start. And then,
after a bit, she'd say, "You haven't said you love me." That
was like taking out the starting-handle when the self-starter
had given up the ghost. "Sure, I've told you that a thousand
times," Johnny would say.

The head book-keeper—an old tartar—interrupted his
meditations.

"Mr Gruntle was looking for you. He said he wanted to
see you when you came in."

"I'll go and see him now." Johnny deliberately played
down the false importance this female tried to attach to her
employer's every whim. She was sex-starved. It was rather
pathetic really. Not every boy of Johnny's age would have
been able to diagnose what was up with the old faggot.

"Ring his secretary first."

"I was going to do that," Johnny said in a drawl. But in
fact he hadn't thought of it.

Mr Gruntle looked up rather testily when Johnny came in.
He had the manner of a man who suffered from piles. It was
very typical of his method to send for Johnny and when he
came to look irritated at the interruption. He also gave the
impression that he wasn't sure who Johnny was.

"Oh, Connolly," he said, "sit down here. I'll be ready to
talk to you in a moment."

Mr Gruntle drove a Mercedes. That was all Johnny knew
about him. There was nothing particularly impressive about
his clothes, and the photographs of his family on the chimney
piece showed only that they were a corny-looking crowd.
There was something unfair about a world that filled the
pockets of such a specimen as Gruntle.

71

He stopped what he was at suddenly and swung round in his chair.

"I was looking for you at 2.45, Connolly. I was told you hadn't come back from lunch."

"That's right. I couldn't get on to a bus; and when at last I managed to, it got caught in a traffic jam in Grafton Street. I'd have been as quick if I'd walked, I declare to God."

"I understand that you haven't been on time for the last fortnight."

"I wouldn't say that quite. I'll admit that I haven't been as punctual sometimes as I'd like to be. From where I live, it is the divil altogether to get into town. But I hope to be moving shortly. It's terrible when you come to think of it to be dependent on public transport."

"Have you thought of getting up half an hour earlier?"

Johnny had a reply to that, but held on to it. Gruntle wasn't going to get a rise out of him.

"I understand from Miss Henshaw that your work is very far from satisfactory."

"I don't know what call she has to say the like of that."

"You were told very plainly that you weren't going to be taken on to the permanent staff unless your performance improved considerably."

"I've done my best; but nobody could work in the conditions I'm expected to put up with."

"The rest of the staff manage to."

"That's not what I hear."

"We are revising the staff list at present, and your name will be coming up for consideration with others."

"If that's the case, Mr Gruntle, may I ask you to let me work in some other end of the business."

"What would you fancy?"

"Something that got me outside a bit. I wouldn't mind being a driver."

"We have all the drivers we need. You were taken into accounts. You made no objection at the time, so far as I can recall."

72

"I didn't know what I was letting myself in for, to be dead honest with you."

"Your work has deteriorated recently, I understand. You are taking no interest in it at all. Jobs are scarce these days. There are many boys who would be grateful for yours."

"Mr Gruntle, I've had trouble at home. My mother isn't well, and I'm thinking of getting married."

Johnny noticed that he had penetrated his employer's hide at last. He shifted in his chair and looked at his clerk with a sudden concentration of interest.

"How old are you?"

"Twenty-one. Well, not exactly. I'll be twenty-one in November."

"And you are thinking of getting married before you have a permanent job. Where will you live?"

"My mother will give us a room while we are waiting for a Corporation flat. There's a waiting list as long as your arm. It's a shame. When you think of the Proclamation of 1916 and all that about 'cherishing all the children of the nation equally'."

"If I were you, I'd postpone my wedding until I got a steady job. And when you get one—if you take my advice—see you put your back into it."

"I'm not being kept on, then?"

"I must be straight with you. You're not."

"I don't think this is fair."

"You've been warned. You've been given every chance. All you have to do is to put accounts into envelopes and tick off the list of debtors. All the rest is done by machines. But even that is too much for you, it seems."

"I'd like to know what fault has been found with my work."

"You put last month's accounts into the envelopes upside down so that the addresses weren't visible. You didn't bother to look at what you were doing. See that."

Mr Gruntle handed Johnny a manilla envelope. The firm's own address peeped through the little plastic window.

"I don't understand," Johnny said. "If they were put in wrong, surely the person who handles the post should have seen it."

"He did."

"Nobody said a word to me about it."

"Miss Henshaw was informed."

"She didn't tell me."

"She told *me*. That's why I sent for you."

"I'd like to talk to Miss Henshaw about this. I mean to say, it isn't fair. Anyone can make a mistake."

"You've been given every chance. Look out for another job. You can stay on until the end of the month. There's nothing for you here, I'm afraid. I'm sorry, Connolly. But perhaps you'll take a pull at yourself now. You'll need to if you want to support a family."

Having nothing else to say, and not wishing Johnny to engage in dialogue, Mr Gruntle made a snapdragon grimace, a smile and dismissal combined, and engrossed himself in the papers on his desk.

Johnny hesitated, and then went out, shutting the door with a fine show of spirit. He was determined to have it out with Miss Henshaw, and expected her to look abashed. But her expression suggested that she knew exactly what had happened, and if Johnny were to raise the issue she would make it clear to all the room that he had been sacked.

As a temporary member of staff he was not a member of a union. Another boy who had been dismissed for punching up the doorkeeper had tried to get the union representative to take up his case and had met with cowardly evasion.

Johnny ignored Miss Henshaw. His best strategy, he decided, was to act as if nothing had happened and at the end of the week to tell his friends that he was leaving of his own accord. They all knew he disliked the work. He felt better when he decided not to knock his head against Miss Henshaw or any other wall.

On the way home he found himself in better spirits than he had been for days. A load had been lifted from his heart.

How mad he had been to think of marrying Lily and walking blindfold into trouble. There was a lot of fun to be found in the world, and he hadn't had his fair share of it yet. There was no need to buy a car at once just because Matt Grimes had one. He would look Matt up, and see if there was an opening for himself in the bookie business.

Lily would be expecting him to say something; but she could go on expecting. There was no reason why he should have to commit himself because she kept on saying "I love you." She was the sort of girl who kept you kissing her long after you'd forgotten she was there. But it was nice having her and not to have to be fishing around for someone. Lily was all right.

His mother was delighted to see him looking so carefree. She hated her boy to be moody. She was afraid that it might spell some new kind of trouble. He was hilarious at tea, couldn't stop talking. Aunt Julia nearly choked in her tea-cup, laughing with him. "I might as well tell her now," Johnny decided. He mightn't be able to pluck up the courage another day.

THE OPEN MIND

T HE SHORT LIST had now been reduced to two, but really, Mr Walpole explained to the board, as a matter of form. Miss Rogers had such outstanding qualifications and seemed in every way so ideally suited to the post that the sub-committee who were making the recommendations would have selected her, if it had not seemed more appropriate to send up the name of the second runner to the board, and let them see what Miss Rogers had up against her before they made the appointment.

Mr Walpole, as usual, had a good deal else to say, but that much was all the board wanted to hear. However, he liked to make himself important on these occasions, and when he took off one just thought of other things until he ran out of steam. Then the chairman put whatever the point of discussion was to the board for decision.

The Barlee Institution had been richly endowed by its founder when he left his small but priceless collection of pictures, furniture and rare books to the public. These were exhibited in the Georgian mansion James Barlee bought for himself shortly before his death; the curator's life was made particularly pleasant because she had the use of the flat Barlee had made snug for himself on the attic floor. Very typical of old Barlee, who was almost aggressively proud of his humble origins, that the residential quarters should have been furnished with the best, most comfortable and practical of modern furniture, and fitted out with every gadget and convenience it was possible to imagine. Culture, he liked to say, was in its own place downstairs. He entertained his friends in his domestic apartments, where there were travel posters on the walls instead of pictures, and conversation consisted of the host's breezy autobiographical monologues. When these were exhausted the guests could play cards or watch television. At ten o'clock everyone was turned out because their host kept regular hours, and was always up by seven, when, if something was on his mind, he thought nothing of calling up an acquaintance on the telephone.

He was essentially a practical man; and he liked to say that everything in his manner of life went to prove it. A childless widower, he kept the ladies who were anxious to console him at bay by a system which withstood every assault. Not that he disliked women; as a practical man he acknowledged their contribution to life, but protected himself against their instinct to attach themselves to a protector. So far was James Barlee from being averse to women that he made it one of the conditions when he negotiated the transfer of his mansion and its contents to a board of eminently respectable trustees that the curator should always be of that sex. Another condition was that no children or animals should be allowed on the premises. In this way the founder made it sufficiently clear what sort of woman he had in mind.

This had all happened in the days when the moral climate in Ireland (where Barlee had settled when he left Australia) was still such as Jane Austen would have recognised. Miss Pratt, the first curator, was a very formidable spinster; the all-male board stood in awe of her. Her efficiency was absolute; her economies iron; her discipline unchallenged.

It was a relief when she was called, as she might have phrased it, to a higher command. Even Walpole, who had acted as her Polonius, relaxed when the board met to discuss a successor. For the first time in their history the trustees smoked; and as if to celebrate the occasion, sweet cakes were provided by the housekeeper with the trustees' cups of tea. In Miss Pratt's time a very plain sort of biscuit had been passed round, refused, and passed round again at the next meeting.

"We will never be able to replace Miss Pratt," Judge

Kennedy said; and his colleagues nodded their agreement. It was necessary to consult the terms of the endowment, which were explained by the solicitor to the trust, who attended for the purpose. He was very helpful about drafting an advertisement for a successor and proposing that applications should be weeded out by three of the trustees, and only the most eligible submitted to the board.

Mr Seal, the solicitor, so capable and useful, marvelled to himself how men who (except for Mr Walpole) made his business so agreeable for him had ever attained their lofty stations in life. The purchase of a doormat could involve the board in an hour's confused discussion, at the end of which it was never quite clear what had been decided; anything more complicated was delegated to a sub-committee.

The relief that the absence of Miss Pratt afforded was soon replaced by a nagging realisation that the duties of the trustees might be more troublesome and time-consuming when her hand was no longer on the tiller. Lord Somerville enjoyed a fantasy of a nymph in attendance at board meetings, but only while the solicitor was being rather boring. When his Lordship roused himself he realised just as well as everyone else that an old dragon like the late lamented saved them all a great deal of trouble.

Curiously enough there was no guide-line for the trustees to follow on the question of age. Any young woman, unless conspicuously repellent, would, by her predecessor's standards, seem frivolous. Women in their middle years give rise to other problems. What was the *right* age for a woman?

"It is unfortunate," Henry Ledbetter was constrained to say, "that we are tied down in this matter to the choice of a woman. There must be any God's quantity of spoilt priests who would be perfectly suited to the job." Henry, as well as being agreeably rich, had acquired a reputation as a humorist and this interjection did not give offence, as it might if anyone else had made it.

"The intentions of the founder," Mr Walpole began . . . Henry could be seen to curse himself for opening the familiar flood-gate. Whatever any of the trustees thought or said, a woman it had to be, and a woman the nature of whose qualifications was left to the judgement of the trustees.

A sub-committee was formed. By tacit consent—he was probably inured to it by now by life experience—Walpole was kept off it. Lord Somerville was on; not Henry (too frivolous); the Judge, of course; and a former bank director, whose opinion was listened to on every subject.

The replacing of Miss Pratt took a considerable time to accomplish. The solicitor would have liked to have gone back to his office with instructions to settle all the business; but some of the trustees (who had very little to do nowadays) thought it necessary to meet again to discuss the final form of the advertisement. There would then follow a period to allow applications to be sent in. Then the preliminary sifting, then, perhaps another meeting, before it was decided whom to invite to meet the sub-committee.

Although it was stipulated in the advertisement that a candidate must have a good university degree, have worked in a museum, be proficient in at least two modern languages and be between the ages of thirty and forty, the flood of applicants that came in included one from an ex-nanny in 'a good family' in her seventieth year, one from a girl of twenty-two who since leaving school had worked in a riding school, and a doctor's widow who had always been fond of sketching until marriage put her hobby out of the question. Each gave as her principal qualification : "I am very fond of reading, but don't get much time." There were many others hardly less absurd; but it was not difficult to reduce the list to half a dozen. Of these, two had recommendations that put them at the head of this list and, after the interview, it was obvious that Miss Rogers was better qualified than Mrs Armstrong. To some extent the first young woman's advantages were due to a more propitious start in life; she had gone to better schools and a more distinguished university, worked in celebrated institutions, travelled, and spoke with authority. Without being conspicuously pretty, she was extremely pleasant to look at; her voice was particularly attractive. She was in her thirty-third year.

"What if she gets married? She's quite nice-looking," the bank man asked his colleagues.

"There is nothing in the rules to forbid it provided she doesn't keep children in the house," the solicitor said (he attended to keep the sub-committee straight).

"Seems rather harsh to me," Lord Somerville intervened. He had taken quite a fancy to Miss Rogers.

"We must abide by the rules," the Judge said.

"I think somebody ought to have a talk with her about this," Lord Somerville continued. He felt suddenly concerned and involved. When he got into a mood of this kind, it brought on a most exasperating habit of ringing up his colleagues for interminable discussions after dinner ('to get my mind easy').

"The advertisement made quite clear that the curator has a residence provided for her, but children and animals are not allowed."

A wrangle then took place : one view was that it should have been stipulated the curator had to be unmarried. But it was the bank director who clinched the argument. Nowadays any effort to confine the post to an unmarried woman would expose the trustees to odium.

It was agreed that nothing would stop Henry Ledbetter quizzing her on the subject when she appeared before the board when they were making the appointment. By this time it was apparent to all the sub-committee that Miss Rogers was way ahead of her only rival Mrs Armstrong, a very worthy person—her career showed what could be achieved by taking advantage of the educational opportunities that were now available to all bright children. But a technical school, and two years in Leeds after a second-class degree from a provincial university, looked very drab beside Miss Rogers's success at Oxford, her stint at the Courtauld Institute, and the years in Paris, Vienna and Florence.

Mrs Armstrong was perfectly civil, thought a long time before answering questions, and did that briefly. She had had to fight her way in the world. That was obvious.

But still, it would have looked high-handed of the sub-committee, having received forty-three applications, to present the board with a *fait accompli*. Better send up the names of the two ladies, and give them the task of making the final obvious choice.

As decent men, they were relieved not to have to bring down the chopper on poor Mrs Armstrong, for whom the free house and furniture would obviously be much more of a boon than for her rival. Miss Rogers had the appearance of someone who had travelled only first class in her young life, and always to pleasant places. It may be taken as the measure of her advantage over her rival that nobody on the sub-committee thought to enquire if there were a Mr Armstrong and, if so, was he going to be included in the package. Nobody saw anyone other than Miss Rogers in Miss Pratt's old position.

But when the names came up before the full board Lord Somerville asked questions about Mr Armstrong—neither of the candidates was present on this occasion, it must be understood. When Miss Rogers was selected she would be invited to meet the board, and it was then that Henry Ledbetter was expected to quiz her in his man-of-the-world way. The chairman became impatient; what did it matter who Mr Armstrong was, or what he did, it was quite irrelevant when his wife wasn't going to get the job.

Had Mr Walpole kept his mouth shut then, all would have been well, but pride of superior knowledge led him to boast that he knew 'something about the background'. Mr and Mrs Armstrong had been fellow students at Liverpool; he worked at book illustrations and did some picture-cleaning on the side. Had he left it at that, no harm would have been done, but Walpole's tongue when off the leash wagged like a puppy's tail. He understood that there was some sort of understanding between the Armstrongs, he said.

"What do you mean exactly?" Lord Somerville got easily bored.

"I think like so many young people nowadays, they are not married officially," Walpole said.

"I would regard that as very much their own business." Lord Somerville sounded severe. He detested cranks and he did not greatly care for Mr Walpole.

"Undoubtedly," Walpole protested. "I mentioned it only incidentally. After all, we must acquaint ourselves with the candidates' backgrounds. I didn't for a moment intend to make any reflection on Mrs Armstrong's domestic arrangements."

All eyes were now turned on the bishop, who had recently been appointed to the board. He tended to go on at too great length about Russian icons of which he possessed an example; otherwise he had shown himself, since he joined the trustees, a model of conciliation. The bishop clearly and understandably would have preferred to keep out of the discussion, but Walpole saw an opportunity to regain ground and exercise his anticlerical muscles.

"If the founder thought we were going to legislate for the private morals of the staff, he would turn in his grave. He was himself extremely liberal in his attitudes; and I, for one, think it our duty not to impose some standard which happens to fit in with our personal codes. I am sure that Miss Pratt was not exposed to cross-examination about *her* private life when she was appointed."

Henry Ledbetter eased the situation with a laugh at this point. Lord Somerville refused to join in.

"I want to hear what the bishop has to say," Mr Walpole persisted.

"So long as the curator does her work and does not allow her domestic concerns to interfere with her duties, I quite agree with Mr Walpole," the bishop said.

Judge Kennedy, who was a Northern Catholic, and rigid in his views, listened with attention to the bishop. Until then he had not let it be seen what view he took, but in the light of what was obviously a concession by the bishop, he must have thought that, if only to support a cleric of his own persuasion, he should commit himself.

"Unless we have information that as trustees it falls within our duties to examine, I don't think we need concern ourselves about Mrs Armstrong's married status. If Mr Walpole's information is correct—"

"I want to make it quite plain that I did not raise this matter with any intention of injuring Mrs Armstrong's application," Mr Walpole burst in. A confirmed agnostic, he was being made to look a bigot by men who believed in miracles.

"Let me finish," the judge proceeded. "I think it is not without relevance to our deliberations that if this lady is— how shall I put it?—in a certain situation—a matter, I agree, that does not immediately concern us—it probably settles the problem we were discussing earlier about children. That rule is binding on us. We have no power to change it."

"There's many a slip—" Henry Ledbetter began, then checked himself.

Today, for some reason, Lord Somerville seemed in no mood for Henry's pleasantries. Usually he enjoyed them, and he invited Henry to his dinners.

"I think," his Lordship said in his most solemn manner, "that we should be very careful to show that we don't hold what Mr Walpole has told the board about her against Mrs Armstrong. I would like to make it quite clear to my colleagues that this matter did not come up for discussion when the sub-committee were making their recommendations to the board. Had it done so I would have followed the line that the bishop and the judge have indicated. I am sorry Mr Ledbetter does not seem to agree with us about the seriousness of the matter."

Henry Ledbetter blushed. "I was merely—" he began, and stopped again in mid-sentence. Somerville was showing a nasty streak that must have lain concealed under that bumble-puppy manner.

"I should certainly not like to seem to stand in the way of any decision the board might think it should come to. I am the most recent member, I don't forget," the bishop said.

"I don't know what has come over us," Lord Somerville said. "Mr Walpole has insisted on introducing a controversial note into an impartial discussion about the merits of two very suitable candidates."

"I protest—" Mr Walpole was on the verge of tears.

"Now that the matter has been raised—and I am quite satisfied that Mr Walpole had no ulterior motive—I think the trustees must consider their position very carefully." Lord Somerville spoke with unusual solemnity. His customary benevolent vagueness was not in evidence now.

"If it gets about that Mrs Armstrong is not legally married and was passed over for that reason, it will lead to a great deal of newspaper discussion. I, for one, think we cannot allow that to happen. Up to now we have kept the business of this institution outside these contentious issues."

"I think we must move cautiously," the former bank director intervened. "From what we have heard Miss Rogers seemed to have been hand-made for the post. But there's an old saying, 'if you want to know me come and live with me'."

At this point, Henry's efforts to catch Lord Somerville's eye failed miserably. He was feeling quite fed up, and asked himself why he remained on this boring board. No salary attached; and the meetings always coincided with some attractive alternative, through some perversity of fate.

"Miss Rogers," the bank director continued, "may not live up to her admittedly hight credentials. She may have some drawback that will come out when it is too late to remedy the situation. With the other lady we know, in a manner of speaking, where we are. She has made her way against difficulties; she must be an extremely hard worker; there are no complaints about her that we are aware of; her duties here are light. The secretary is quite capable of doing them unaided. All in all, I would say we were very lucky in finding a candidate so well-fitted for the post, and if it were not that

Miss Rogers is so much better qualified we would have been very glad to appoint Mrs Armstrong without further discussion. If I may make one more point—I won't keep you long. While I fully support all that has been said about our duty not to hold against Mrs Armstrong what some of us might regard as a social handicap, there is a practical side to it which won't escape your attention. She will be contented. She is less likely to find the rather remote situation irksome. I have nothing more to say."

When Lord Somerville made another speech, repeating, as was his way, word for word what the bank director had just said, and Mr Walpole, not to be outdone, spoke of intimidation (and glanced at the bishop), Henry Ledbetter checked himself. He had been about to say that nothing altered the fact that Miss Rogers was the best qualifed candidate, but the atmosphere in the boardroom was muffled with unanimity; it required more moral energy than Henry Ledbetter had on tap to disturb it; and he was at that moment more concerned with his reactions to his colleagues that the appointment of a stranger to a sinecure. The crank usually amused him; he was so marvellously predictable; but today he had been tiresome, and Somerville was obviously nettled. Somerville's expression when he looked at Miss Rogers's photograph had amused Henry. He took a second look at it after it went round the table when he thought nobody was noticing. That was when it was clear her appointment was a matter of form. But since then he had worked himself into a thoroughly disagreeable humour. Pompous at all times, he had become unbearably so, and had put Henry out of countenance twice. Henry was a bit of a performer, he knew it and everyone knew it; but it helped to lighten these occasions, and he provided light relief. He was most anxious to get back into Somerville's good books. Memories of many pleasant evenings came to mind. None of these other fellows had any part in them. God forbid!

"We are taking a long time to come to a decision, my Lord Bishop, my Lord and gentlemen," the chairman said.

He spoke like that with only seven of them there (and the solicitor, of course). Walpole, who had been twitching like mad during the discussion, and was determined to rehabilitate himself, leaped into action and proposed Mrs Armstrong.

"I'll second that," said Somerville. Then he looked at Henry Ledbetter disapprovingly, but it might well have been self-consciously. How is one to tell? Henry's impulse was to please. "I'll support that," he said.

"I will go with my colleagues," said the bishop. Judge Kennedy nodded his head enigmatically.

"And what about you, Judge?" the chairman asked.

"I'm not objecting," he said.

It only remained for the bank director. His nod was accepted by the chairman without a question.

The secretary was instructed to inform the candidates of the result and to summon Mrs Armstrong to attend at a date to be fixed to meet the board.

There was about all the men as they came out the aura of having had business to do and having done it—an expression of well-being and achievement and brotherhood in achievement. They parted with mutual expressions of goodwill. Henry was thwarted in an effort to have a private word with Somerville. Walpole had his Lordship by the top button and only let go when his captive risked losing it and plunged into his car.

That evening, after dinner, Henry's wife told him that he was wanted on the telephone: Lord Somerville.

"I've just been going through the copies of the applications that the secretary sent us. How did we come to appoint Mrs Armstrong? Miss Rogers had infinitely better qualifications. There should have been no question. How do you account for it? If Miss Rogers were to complain, I for one would be at a loss for an explanation. What possessed us?"

"I was going to vote for Miss Rogers until Walpole proposed the other woman and you seemed so convinced she was the more suitable, I didn't want to queer your pitch."

"There was no question of queering *my* pitch. What I'm

exercised about is the injustice we seem to have done to this young Rogers woman. I can't understand it. Surely the solicitor should have said something. After all, he is paid. It's his job."

"Let's be fair to Seal. He's only our lawyer. I think you would be the first to object if he usurped the functions of the trustees."

"I agree. I wasn't being quite fair. Mr Seal is very helpful and attentive. But what happened to us? There was far too much talking for one thing. I hate that. One gets so confused."

"Walpole caused all the mischief. He is such a tiresome creature, with nothing whatever to do. He brought up this question about Mrs Armstrong's boy-friend. I must say I was surprised to find the bishop and old Kennedy so permissive."

"Of course I was very much concerned that there should be no discrimination of any kind."

"Very right of you, if I may say so. We were all anxious to support you on that. I think that's where we allowed ourselves, perhaps, to be carried away."

"It is certainly an extraordinary business. I'm upset about it. I wish you had spoken up. You always bring in a refreshing note of common sense. It's such a relief when one has had to put up with the nonsense that little lunatic, Walpole, goes on with. How did he ever get on to the board?"

"A mistake."

"It certainly was."

"Miss Pratt landed him on us. He knows a great deal about the history of wallpaper. That impressed her. None of us knew him unfortunately."

"You weren't on the sub-committee. We were all charmed by Miss Rogers. The other woman is very dour and not nearly so accomplished. I suppose we can't do anything about it now."

"I'm afraid not. I'm sure Miss Rogers will get another post. The Institute is at the back of beyond. She would have been bored to death."

"We could have entertained her. She would have been a welcome change after her predecessor. *De mortuis*, however. Well, I'm glad to have had this chat. There's nobody else on the board I can let my hair down with. I thought you were not your usual cheerful self today. Nothing the matter I hope? Family all well?"

"Fine, thank you. I was in good form until we got bogged down in that discussion. I wish there were some way to shut that old fellow up. If only he had kept his mouth shut today."

"Well, all we can do is to keep our mouths shut. I hope this doesn't get about. We would look very foolish."

"The great thing is, anyone could do the job."

"Yes. That's a comfort. You never fail me, Henry. Trust you to see the situation in perspective. I worry too much."

"What did *he* want?" Mrs Ledbetter enquired when her spouse returned.

"There was a rather pretty girl up for the job. And she didn't get it. Largely because of his interference. Now he's sorry about it. Thinks he may have been unjust. She was far the better qualified of the two, as it happens."

"I think it may be just as well," Mrs Ledbetter said. "That coffee's cold. I'll make you some more."

KILDONAN'S HOPE

M R F I T Z P A T R I C K H A D called to discuss the terms
of a lease. He was in the carrying business. On his way out
he stopped to have a word with Michael in the general office.

"I hear you are thinking of getting married," Mr Fitzpatrick said.

"I'm three months married," Michael replied, surprised it
didn't show.

"Then it isn't too late to wish you luck."

"Thank you." And then, because it was the only topic he
had ever discussed with him, Michael enquired after Mr
Fitzpatrick's horse.

"The mare is in splendid form. Never saw her better.
Eating her head off. She's running at the Park on Saturday.
She ought to be worth a couple of quid."

"Do you really fancy her?" There was a shade of un-
easiness in the younger man's voice. He had undermined a
recent resolve by asking the question.

"She's in very well at the weights. She ought to beat what
she's up against on Saturday. But you know what racing is."

Michael knew only too well. If in the past he could have
disciplined his ardour and confined his betting to opportunities like this where he was getting information out of the
horse's mouth, what a rewarding hobby racing might have
been; but he had never been able to confine himself to
occasional bets. The bustle of a racecourse mesmerised him;
even the faint far hum of bookmakers giving tongue acted
on his blood like benzedrine. He was virtually neighing when
he arrived on the course.

A week ago, after losing two months' salary at the Curragh

—all would have been saved if the jockey in the last race had concentrated on his business and not looked over his shoulder to see where the others were—a week ago he had sworn to Milly he would give racing up.

Michael found that he could think of nothing but the subject of his conversation with Mr Fitzpatrick. The business of the office clients became as trivial as it was irrelevant. Kildonan's Hope—he knew and respected her, an animal whose full potential had probably not yet been realised. Her owner, temperamentally at the furthest pole from Michael, raced this mare for pleasure. He had bred her on his farm, and was satisfied when she paid for her keep by winning more races than she lost, always running gamely, never being asked to exert herself unduly. Mr Fitzpatrick, a modest, self-sufficient, comfortable citizen, was eaten up by no ambition to win the Grand National, for instance. His goals were more easily attainable. When Kildonan's Hope ran on Saturday his owner would bet perhaps as much as twenty-five pounds on her chances, certainly not more, and be neither elated if he won nor cast down if he lost. His interest was centred on the mare. An unimpassioned concern in comparison with the picture that arose like Faust's vision of Helen before Michael's inward eye. He saw first the green sward and the white enclosing rails; then, like a sheet of flame, the mingled colours of the jockeys' shirts swept into view as they wheeled round the last bend and into the broad straight ribbon of turf that led to the winning-post and the stands, half a mile away.

Now the horses were approaching head on, and he could pick out the individual colours of their riders. Red in front, followed by green, followed by black and white, and behind them an indistinguishable cluster. Now the red falls back; now the black and white joins the green. They come bearing down on Michael, locked together. But a roar from the crowd signals the appearance on the far side of the course, racing by herself, of a small mare that has come from nowhere and is now moving like a laser beam. The colours are

indistinct—muddy mauve or some mixture of that shade—
but the mare identifies herself. How often had Kildonan's
Hope borne down on her rivals like this and swept past them
in one long sustained joyous rush.

Now she is past the post; her jockey is sitting up; the
momentum of that final burst of speed carries the mare out
of sight behind the stands, leaving the horses who seemed to
be making such a brave show before she challenged them
to struggle wearily for the honour of second and third places.
Michael switched his mental camera from the racecourse to
the rail where the bookmakers cowered as he descended on
them like a fox on a hen-roost. A huge, a final killing. Their
satchels, plump before, hung limply like punctured bladders
after he had done with them. When Kildonan's Hope won,
the odds were always rather liberal because the owner was
not a gambler, and as he trained the mare himself there was
no stable money on her to depress the odds. She would
probably win at three to one.

Michael lost five hundred pounds the afternoon he re-
nounced racing for ever. That had been sacrified in an effort
to recover one hundred lost on the previous Saturday at
Naas in an effort to recover the fifty pounds lost on the
Saturday before that at Leopardstown.

He drew a line across the record when he married. Without renouncing racing—Milly enjoyed the afternoon's outing—he had come to an understanding with himself that
marriage could not be maintained if he continued to contribute such a large share of his income to the turf. "I must
go easy" is how he put it. Milly was unaware of the extent
and scope of his betting. But he found the wagering of small
sums so insipid that he was bored, and even Milly's company
did not redeem the afternoon from triviality. He should
have stayed away. But what was there to do on a Saturday
afternoon if you didn't go to the races? Nobody had sup-
plied Michael with a satisfactory answer to that question.

At the races, on the next occasion, having played with a
few pounds all day he happened to be standing beside a

bookmaker when he was taking a bet of three hundred pounds to fifty. It sounded sumptuous. A nod of the head, that was all that was required—Michael had an account with the bookmaker—and three hundred pounds would be his in less than five minutes (the horses were in their stalls at the starting gate). He nodded.

Belisarius, as the horse was called, had no appetite for racing that day. He came from a powerful stable, and if his trainer fancied him the odds would have been even money. Whoever put fifty pounds on at six to one had money to throw away. These were the things Michael told himself on the slow drive home. He was angry with the man who had made the original bet, as a professional is angry when he sees an untrained slovenly performance. But his anger with the oaf was as nothing compared with his rage with himself for having been so easily seduced by bad example. He hadn't used his brain at all; he was on a par with a maiden lady picking out her fancy with a pin. He was ashamed of himself. The lapse told him that he had deteriorated from lack of practice. It was in the spirit of a puritan that he went to the races at Naas with the intention of recovering the fifty pounds so wantonly thrown away. After that he would tell Milly that they must devise some other way of spending Saturday afternoons. A close study of the card told him that there was one certain way to win back his fifty pounds. Of the four runners in the last race, Parnell, who would almost certainly start at short odds, could hardly fail to win. When they arrived at the course Michael avoided his usual aquaintances and spent most of the afternoon on top of the stand. Milly had never seen this side of his nature. "I like just to sit here in the sunshine," he said. She had on a new dress, and would have liked to show it off; but it was a small sacrifice in return for her husband's undivided attention. At race meetings, he neglected her, giving all his mind to the business in hand.

After the fifth race Michael left Milly and came down from the stand. He took up a position beside a bookmaker. When the prices were chalked up tentatively—three to one the field and even money Parnell—Michael put a hundred pounds on the favourite.

Milly, to whom he had made another excuse for his withdrawal, was waiting for him when he came back. Now that he had put the money on Parnell, the chances of his being beaten began to present themselves in vivid colours. He was carrying top weight; the ground was heavy after rain; Tim Healy, a younger horse, getting weight for age, looked an extremely attractive proposition at three to one. Milly noticed that Michael had lost his love of nature and the open air during his absence. He had become his usual brooding preoccupied self. "Shall I put a tenner on Tim Healy, as a saver, just in case?" he was asking himself. In that event he might, more logically, put twenty on that animal and another ten on Parnell. That would be an investment of eighty pounds more than he had intended; but it seemed improvident to risk all on Parnell. Michael's faith in him had by this time dwindled, and he was asking himself why he had been so confident that this favourite presented the solution to his problem. Milly said something to him. He wasn't paying attention. She pouted. He wished he had stayed at home and written off his losses.

Still uncertain, and harassed now by Milly sulking at his side, he did nothing to mend his hand. He stayed to watch Tim Healy win by several lengths. Parnell, setting off behind the other horses, seemed satisfied to remain in that position throughout.

'Buying money' is the expression used for the way in which Michael set about recouping the one hundred and fifty pounds lost, as he saw it, through carelessness and indecision. An unbeaten two-year-old, already being backed for next year's Derby, was due to run on the following Saturday. The bookmakers offered odds calculated to discourage all but the desperate. Michael put on five hundred pounds to win two hundred, giving him back his losses with a small bonus. This was the occasion when the jockey looked back to see how far he was ahead of his rivals, giving one of them a chance to sneak up and beat him by a short head. After that Michael made a full confession. He had to because the only way to pay his betting bill was to sell the motor car his father-in-law had given them as a wedding present. Milly took the blow badly.

"I am sick and tired of racing," she said. "Even our honeymoon had to be dedicated to it. I never thought when you said you would take me to Paris that it meant going to race meetings every day. What am I going to say to Daddy?"

"You know I wouldn't sell the car if I could get the money any other way," Michael said.

Milly then offered to sacrifice her engagement ring. As Michael had economised over that article, being under pressure at the time, he was now in a quandary. Milly, fortunately, was a romantic-minded girl and believed him when he said that death would be preferable. They were still debating the problem—the car had not yet been sold—when Mr Fitzpatrick, unbidden, told Michael to back Kildonan's Hope.

Michael had decided, among other things, in future to open his mind to Milly, to share his secrets with her. So long as he did that, he could not be tempted into wrong courses. Had he always taken her into his confidence he wouldn't be in this mess. "We must have no secrets from each other," he said. Milly, touched by his sentiment when her ring was in danger, showed a tendency to forgive.

"I'll be glad to get away from the old racing," she said. "You've no idea how dull it is to spend the evenings with a man who can't take his nose out of the form book. You must take up gardening," she decided.

Drying the dishes while she did the washing up, after their evening meal, Michael made a casual reference to Mr Fitzpatrick's call. "Just my luck. If this had happened even a week ago, we would not be in trouble now. Why must he come along and tell me about this animal when it's too late, when I've given up betting? There's all the difference in the world between betting on a tip from a man like that and putting one's money on a horse because the odds suggest that it is being backed by the stable. One's a certainty, the other's only guess-work."

He was hoping Milly would remind him that it was not too late, even now, and that Mr Fitzpatrick's appearance at this moment should be seen as the intervention of Providence. If she saw it that way, she did not say so.

Michael continued: "I don't think anyone knows quite how good this animal is. If she were in one of the big stables where there is trial tackle we would have some idea; but as it is Fitzpatrick is satisfied to let her run in these potty little races where she meets nothing capable of extending her. There is something very attractive about his amateur approach—he quite genuinely races her for the fun of the thing—but it is a pity to see a good animal being wasted. If she were mine I'd try to persuade Vincent O'Brien to train her. But, of course, the top trainers aren't interested in small fry, people with only one horse. I suppose Mr Fitzpatrick is doing the right thing if he wishes simply to enjoy himself. He never told me to back Kildonan's Hope before, by the way. The furthest he ever went on other occasions was to say 'I think she'll give them a gallop', or 'I shouldn't be surprised if she ran well'. This time he was quite emphatic."

Michael broke off. He was getting no encouragement. Milly's refusal to contribute to the conversation, and the way in which she stared at each plate before she washed it unnerved him. He found himself listening to his own voice, and was not impressed by the sound.

"I'll go to the bank tomorrow. The manager might increase my overdraft. I believe money is not as tight as it was; but if he wants me to pay it back in a year, say, what can I do? I don't suppose your brother would lend it to you?"

"I'd rather sell the car," Milly said.

"It would only be for a year at most. I intend to put away

fifty pounds a month out of my salary until we are in the clear."

"And how are we going to manage on what's left, I'd like to know?"

"In that case, we might as well part with the car. We can always tell your father that we couldn't afford to run it. That's true, as a matter of fact."

"Daddy's no fool. I suppose everyone knows you bet beyond your means. I'll tell him the truth. If I don't, you may be sure someone else will."

"Wouldn't it be more sensible to wait until after Saturday and take a chance with Fitzpatrick's mare? I'm sure I'll get three to one if I jump in early with my bet. We only need six hundred and fifty. Supposing I put three hundred on: that pays every penny I owe the books and leaves us two and a half hundred profit. We could do with it if we are going to Madeira in September. I'm not rushing into this. I've been doing a lot of quiet thinking. If we leave things as they are and sell the car, your father will never feel the same towards me again. He will get the impression that his daughter has married a waster. I don't like the sound of that. Suppose the worst happens; suppose by some miracle Kildonan's Hope gets beaten, we will then owe nine fifty; but looked at from your father's point of view—he is accustomed to dealing with large sums, remember—there isn't all that amount of difference between six fifty and nine fifty. In either case we are up against it. And if you want to know my real opinion—I think if your father were to hear that Mr Fitzpatrick gave us this chance of getting out of our troubles, and we from pure cussedness refused to take it, I don't think he would be grateful. I wouldn't be if I were in his shoes."

Milly refused to support Michael's reasoning; but she neither wanted to part with the car nor have to tell her father the reason why. She had her pride. She was tempted to call on Mr Fitzpatrick without letting Michael know; but decided that would not be good for his reputation as a lawyer. She was young and still in love if sadly disillusioned

—she gave her consent, ungraciously, at last. When Saturday came Michael went to the races by himself. To be with him Milly decided would be as pleasurable as being present when he was undergoing a surgical operation. Kildonan's Hope was running in the third race.

"I'll come away immediately after the race," he promised, "whether or not she wins."

He hadn't appeared at a race meeting by himself since he married. Old friends who had been accustomed to drinking with him at the bar between races were glad to see him looking like a bachelor again. He warmed to their welcome and struggled against a good-natured impulse to share his secret. Once his money was on, he would pass the news round; but not until then.

Drinking at the bar before the first race with one of his oldest racing acquaintances, he saw him step aside and exchange a few words with a dwarf. "You must forgive me," he said when he returned. "That was Micky Scott, the best man to ride a two-year-old that I have ever seen. He's helping an American widow with her stud. He tells me that their filly has a stone in hand in this race. She never ran before; but they have a line through another of their string who ran a blinder at the Curragh. I'm going to get my money on before there's a run on her."

As he spoke, he opened his race card and pointed an urgent finger at Primula, the last runner in the list. Michael was impressed by his friend's demeanour. He had passed on this valuable information without any pomposity of reflected glory; without an air of feverish excitement; but as one who knew his business to another who respected and understood it. A fine type, this Hailey, and one who kept his own counsel. His letting Michael into a secret was not only friendly, it was a rare compliment. From an older and more experienced punter, a gesture of recognition. Michael felt a glow. He needed encouragement. No man is the better for having fallen in his wife's esteem. Suppose Kildonan's Hope were to lose, suppose for a moment that catastrophe took

97

place—would it not seem obvious then that if the risk could have been spread over other horses or, at least, one other horse that it was reckless not to seize the opportunity? This was not gambling : this was insurance.

When he came out of the bar into the sunshine and saw Primula written up with a large 8 chalked beside it, he invested fifty pounds at once and only just in time. The odds were halved. The news had gone around.

Primula was unlucky not to win. There was nothing wrong with the tip except that it left out of account her maiden disposition. Never again would she swerve like that when the jockey touched her with his whip. Next time she would be paying attention. Hailey, like the good fellow he was, sought Michael out after the race, full of contrition.

"You saw yourself what happened. She's green. But I think she will get us back our money next time. Unfortunately, after that display, she will never be allowed to run at such a splendid price. I hope you didn't plunge. There is always a risk at the first appearance on a racecourse. Duggan tells me his old horse can't be beaten in this race, by the way, but I'm afraid the bookies know it too. If you hurry, you may still get even money."

Michael put on enough to get back what he shouldn't have lost over the first race. It was a pity Duggan's horse rapped himself going into the starting stall. No horse can run on three legs.

A man of poorer character than Hailey would have avoided Michael after that; but he was thoroughly sincere and attached in his bluff way to the young lawyer who seemed so helpless in these surroundings. His sympathy was very necessary at the moment. Michael's bookmaker had unnerved him by his manner when he took the last bet. There was something in the expression of the eye that was not out of plumb that suggested he was doubting his client's ability to pay.

Michael had no intention of borrowing from Hailey, but he felt the need of a friend. He told him as briefly as possible what his situation was. This involved giving Hailey the tip, but then Hailey had given him two. It was a fair exchange.

Hailey listened attentively. Then he said : "Kildonan's Hope is a courageous little animal, but if you have noticed she never wins on a right-hand course. There are some horses like that. It must have something to do with their sense of balance. Another thing, I know for a fact that Johnny Roe was offered the mount and turned it down. He's riding Rachel's Bower, and I understand she's going to be a very short-priced favourite. You can't afford to take a risk. If I were you I'd put something on Kildonan's Hope—whatever happens she will be trying—but put as much as you can afford on Roe's mount. When Johnny fancies a horse as much as that he never makes a mistake."

Grateful for a friend when he was a prey to indecision, Michael went out to face the odd-eyed bookmaker. Whatever that worthy's private misgivings, he accepted a bet of two hundred pounds on the favourite and five pounds on Kildonan's Hope—a gesture of loyalty—at six to one.

"I hope you helped yourself," Mr Fitzpatrick said to Michael when they happened to meet in the lavatory after the race.

"Thank you very much; and heartiest congratulations," Michael replied. He had lost his money; he still kept his manners. And if he avoided Hailey, it was asking a great deal of anyone in the circumstances to keep entirely civil.

Milly was watching at the window. "Did it win ?"

"Yes," her husband said, brushing past her. She heard the door of what in play they called his study crash open and shut with a bang.

HARRY

HARRY HAS BEEN around since the very beginning, making a nuisance of himself, looking for attention and sulking when he doesn't get it, overwhelmed by trifles; but his worst feature, which has caused him to interfere most disastrously in what might otherwise have been a pleasant and useful life, is his gross and vulgar intrusion at precisely the moment when I am negotiating the most delicate contracts where tact and moderation are essential. When I say 'vulgar' —an imprecise word which is enlisted by opposing camps— I may give a misleading impression.

Harry would be astonished to be so described; he has seen himself so often on the side of the angels, and as he has grown older has become increasingly pompous. He is vulgar when he is most insensitive, and a bore of heroic proportions when his over-thin skin is punctured. How often I have been on the brink of perfect rapport with a sympathetic soul when Harry has come bustling in with some Othello tale of his accomplishments. Once started, nothing will stop him; afterwards, when I remonstrate with him, he pleads nervousness or fatigue or says he got simply carried away. And I can't shake him off. As soon as I realised how much irreparable damage he had done me, I squared up to him. I refused to listen to his excuses, and when he said I was ungrateful, that all his efforts were made exclusively *on my account*, I quoted Johnson's remark to the hardly less adhesive Boswell : "Sir, you have but two topics, yourself and me, I am sick of both."

The trouble is that Harry is now too old, his arteries have hardened; try as he may, it is too late to hope for any permanent improvement, he makes an effort occasionally, but I can't rely on him. If he is not under my eye he will always let me down in an emergency. I have learned that. Our private talks, my remonstrances, his abject tears and heartfelt promises—all a waste of time, and they leave me in the very condition in which I am least able to restrain him before the damage is done.

Why did I not part with him long ago? An obvious question, to which the answer is that he was comfortably installed before I had the wit to recognise him as an impostor. He used to act as if he were a surrogate conscience. At times he has convinced *me* that I was dependent on *him*. His effrontery hasn't stopped there; he is persuaded that any success we have when we go out together is due to his taking over completely. I might as well not be there. If only he knew how fatuous he looks, like a child at its own birthday party. He never forgets to remind me that any success I may enjoy is due exclusively to my connection with him. Whenever I have been involved in any business particularly close to my heart I have noticed that he is very much in the ascendant while the matter is moving, but when it is finished he makes sure to unload a cargo of woe on my doorstep.

What has my wife to say about all this? Why has she not done something to help me to escape from the man who has distorted my life? No one has had such a vantage point. She sees Harry at close range. He will literally take the house over when he thinks he is in the driving seat. I am sorry for her on these occasions. At first she used to look to me for help, but very soon discovered that I am mesmerised by Harry. He has taken charge before I am alive to what is going on. And if I struggle with him then—as I have proved by experience —I can only win by humiliating him before witnesses. Afterwards, in private, at night, he takes it out on me. So I pretend I don't notice. Many a spouse will sympathise with me. I've seen them sitting there, with expressionless faces, while their mate is giving a routine performance. Sometimes, I suppose, one of them, afterwards, says, "That must be the tenth time you told the Browns that story," or whatever. And then the row that was avoided at the party begins. There is no victory in these wars. *Détente* is the wise policy. There is *détente* between me and Harry and *détente* between me and my wife and *détente* between my wife and Harry. It breaks down sometimes.

Once, when I tried to explain to my wife that I wasn't aware of the menace Harry would prove to our marriage (there was no question of moving him out. He was attached to the premises) she surprised me by informing me—quite calmly—that she had been alive to the danger from the beginning; but she was so infatuated with me and so over-awed by him at the time that she had put up with the situation. She thought I was worth whatever Harry deducted as his percentage from our happiness. Besides, she was so inexperienced that she could convince herself I would never have installed him so comfortably had I not some advantage to gain from the association. She had been deeply hurt when she discovered Harry had insisted on coming with us on the honeymoon. She stared at me uncomprehendingly as if she was asking herself was this the man she had fallen in love with? Our compromise began then. Harry did not quite manage to wreck our fortnight in the Dolomites. The air and the exercise agreed with him so well, he was often asleep when his presence would have been embarrassing for me, intolerable for her.

I think she learnt that if our marriage was to work she would have to accommodate herself to Harry's vagaries. If he hasn't quite succeeded in wrecking our marriage it is entirely due to her forbearance. She treats him as one of the family. So much so that sometimes I wonder if she has for-gotten me. Life is organised to suit his whims. And he has the grace to acknowledge this. The rows in our house are all between Harry and me. My wife remains aloof. I don't come out of this well. I have taken advantage of my wife's patience. Visitors to our house are surprised to see how well she seems to get on with Harry who, needless to say, usurps my functions as a host. The impression we give is of a happy home in which Harry does all the talking, and the rest of us are content to listen and prompt when the exuberance of his own verbosity intoxicates him. I am lost to shame; I accept her sacrifice without acknowledgment. I can even—to head off despair—persuade myself that she has begun to enjoy his brazen performance. Habit in the long run is stronger than reason. I did try in the beginning when I saw how unhappy he was making her—he hardly ever left us alone—I did try to point out to him that there wasn't room for the three of us and that if he didn't go, she would move out. And then it would be too late. It is the measure of his ascendency that it did not occur to me even then to threaten to move out with her, leaving Harry in the lurch.

I expected him to become indignant, and I prepared myself for a contest, but to my astonishment he became at once all concern. There was nothing, he said, in which he took such pride as my marriage. Had I ever discovered the part he had played in bringing it about? Who provided the feathers I displayed to such advantage when I went courting? Who dictated the letters that intrigued her? Who suggested the idea of pretending that I had sent Miriam Higgins packing when the fact was I had been pursuing her for years without so far having succeeded in getting so much as a card at Christmas? At the most important stage of my life, he had been inconspicuously at my elbow. I had been too bewitched to notice; I had lulled myself into believing I was dictating strategy when the truth was—and I had better face it now—he had engineered the whole business.

It took me a long time to recover from this revelation. I should have rounded on him then, but I let the poison work in my system. I began to see that Harry had been much more in evidence at the time of my engagement than I realised. Because he was connected with me she liked him. And, of course, I was delighted to show him off. Had she been more critical in the beginning we might between us have done something to control him. But she was hypnotised by him. I can see that now and—it is mortifying to have to admit it—the glamour of Harry was more than half my attraction. By myself I am unsure and self-conscious—Miriam Higgins saw through Harry at once, and when she refused to have him around when we went out together I was as impressive as a battery hen.

Harry is too much for me. I can neither live with him nor without him. And he is so plausible when he wants to get his way. Now I can see only too plainly that he is preparing to take over the liquidation of my marriage. He will justify this by presenting an unpaid bill for having arranged it in the first place. He won't make a crude demand. That is not the way he proceeds. He is too subtle for that. He hints, and leaves me to decode the message. Often I get it wrong, and when it suits him he takes advantage of these mistakes. Oh, he is cunning. He reminds me of the tragedies of my early existence—he has them off by heart and recites them as might a nun a decade of the rosary—seducing me by a process which is so subtle and disarming that I am persuaded for the time being (all he is concerned with) that I have no wiser or, certainly, more sympathetic friend. The damage Harry does when he takes the rôle of relief officer is incalculable, not so much on account of the effectiveness of the disguise (sharp people have seen through it) but because he not only fools me, but anyone else who happens to be close to me at the moment and in a receptive mood.

The first time I suffered seriously at Harry's hands was when I applied for a post in a provincial gallery, exactly what I had been looking out for since I missed a First (Harry comes into that story) and had to give up the idea of the Foreign Service. The interviewing committee had been encouraging —I did very well without the support Harry thinks he gives me—they didn't attach much importance to the sore subject of my second-class degree—they were quietly impressed by my general knowledge of painting (I don't pretend to be a universal expert)—nobody had tested the extent of my aquaintance with the modern languages I had rather rashly claimed—and that ghastly year in Christie's was taken at its face value. I could see the interviewers glancing at one another with that expression which says 'we needn't look any further than this', and I began to think the job was in the bag when Harry surfaced. Don't ask me from where. He had come to explain that I was ill on the day that I sat for my degree, and that anyhow Kenneth Clark hadn't got a First and (with a giggle) 'had done pretty well without it'. And, as if that wasn't enough, he asked permission to suggest some improvements that should be effected at once if the gallery was to be run efficiently. Before he had got half-way, I could see what was happening; but I was powerless to stop him, and I suppose one idiot half of me thought after he began that I might have been too sanguine. Perhaps I needed to strengthen my claim.

But now I could see that the ground I had made was being given back in clumsy handfuls. The encouraging expression I had seen in the chairman's face was replaced by the artificial smile of a sleeping crocodile. One of the panel yawned; another stared at his watch; the *coup de grâce* was given by a spinster of a certain age who had looked on me not unkindly before this lunatic intrusion. "Mr Chairman," she said, "I'm afraid time is running out if we are to see the other candidates before lunch."

"Thank you very much," the chairman said, opening his eyes suddenly. "We have your address; the secretary will write and notify you of our decision."

I tried to dissociate myself from Harry as I slunk out of the room. He knew what he had done. The damn fellow never needs to be told. He was profuse in regrets and apologies; and then tried to put the blame on the woman, to whose unmarried condition he made unbecoming references, as if that made my humiliation any easier to bear. I was too deep in despair even to try to answer him (she was sour-looking, I must admit). I had no desire to punish Harry. I wanted only never to see him again. I didn't have to tell him. But we knew, both of us, that it was hopeless. At the precise moment when I had persuaded myself that I had given him the slip for good—if that was during some delicate crisis in my affairs when the intrusion of an outsider would be fatal—that awful, that inevitable voice would be heard, and I would stand helpless and watch the golden moment fade.

Long ago I gave up trying to restrain him, much less to escape from him, and am humbly grateful when he leaves me alone. But he enlisted a useful ally in boredom. I still call him to relieve it, and the cost is always ruinous.

When I have work on hand, he keeps to his own quarters, and I forget about his wretched existence. He comes in fussing, of course, as soon as I have completed it. To observe him then can be amusing, if you haven't to accept responsibility for his antics, as I must. He is not much impressed by my own estimate of my performance; all he needs is some hint that it may have some merit so that he won't injure his own reputation by association. Given the least encouragement by me he goes off in search of a critic whose good opinion may be quoted. In the critic's presence he invariably puts on a show of diffidence. If the verdict is unfavourable, he has several escape hatches in readiness for a swift retreat; the one most favoured is to say that he had thought as much and only sought to have his opinion confirmed.

Depending on several factors, he may abandon the promotion at the stage before he has done any harm; but more probably he will brood over the reverse and try to think of a reason for doubting the validity of the first critic's opinion. It might, for instance, have been influenced by jealousy or some irrelevant personal consideration, or he might not have given the matter the full attention it deserved. He may then go through the same motions with a second critic; and on this occasion will be alert to withdraw quickly if his reception is unpromising. Then he will almost certainly abandon the enterprise; but in the small hours his rest will be disturbed by the humiliating possibility of the critics meeting and comparing notes.

Hunger for praise makes him take risks; and it is ludicrous

sometimes to see him come forward and step back in almost the same movement. When praise comes unsolicited he positively glows; but Harry is unable to enjoy accomplishment without an audience. He must spread the news. He will sometimes go to pains to let this seem to happen by accident—an open book on a table. His temperament won't let him wait for the fish to bite. Recklessly he will plunge in to see, regardless of the dampening possibilities. He has never learned that he does me most harm when he goes pushing my successes under people's noses, pointing out paragraphs in newspapers, showing letters. Never by any chance containing unfavourable comments—I was going to say that, but it does Harry's common sense too much justice. He is quite capable of sharing a setback with some preoccupied and uninterested stranger, and, of course, always with my wife. In her case he waits until she inquires the reason for his doomsday look. He knows he might wait for ever for a similar enquiry at work, where his depressed moods, when noticed, are resented.

Perhaps I am not being strictly fair to Harry. He has a jolly, an ebullient, even a magnanimous side to his character. I can never keep up, much less compete with him when these are on display. But I must say this for him : he responds to kindness. I have never known—I cannot conceive—a more impressionable disposition. He has collected friends and admirers, but keeps them only on condition that he is economical of their time. How often I have seen a relationship which began in full bloom wither rather rapidly because he has forgotten this. His attentions are as excessive as his neglects are gross. And his efforts to pretend that anyone else could be the centre of interest always break down. In the rôle of an audience he is never convincing; and all too complacently assumes that his superficial performance will be accepted indefinitely as a fair exchange for the attention he is given when on stage.

Harry is always ready with sympathy; he flatters himself that his character is essentially compassionate. The state of the world depresses him whenever it is brought to his notice.

He would like to wipe out human suffering with one grand gesture, and then concentrate on himself who cannot be disposed of so unceremoniously.

When Harry hears a tale of woe, his attention is alerted at once; he usually interrupts it before the close, not to change the subject, but in order to provide an analogous example within his own experience. As to alms-giving, he is in constant difficulties; he doesn't like to part, having always some need for money, but he likes the feeling of benevolence. When I least want to do it, he urges me to act the philanthropist. And as soon as I have obeyed him, as likely as not he will think of some enterprise that promises enjoyment and blame *me* for having been so improvident.

I made a serious gaffe when I drew his attention to the character of Malvolio in *Twelfth Night*. The allusion was untactful, and I had no sooner made it than I regretted it. Harry was not flattered—he takes umbrage and gets down-hearted very easily—but he was at pains to point out to me that Malvolio was essentially a tragic character.

That is the sort of paradox that would appeal to him; intended of course to draw my attention to the fact that he was a tragic character himself *au fond*. I have noticed an ever-growing tendency in him after any setback to rush to the opposite extreme and assume the character of his rival. When he finds himself not in the right and realises that the fact is known, he is not content to be an ordinary defaulter or to accept any routine punishment. Because he is not the beloved disciple, then he must take on himself the sin of Judas. No outer circle of Hell for him. His place everywhere is at the centre. He has a very ample sense of the amount of misery he is causing by failing to be present on any occasion. If the occasion is a very grand or a very humble one his remorse is quite extraordinary. Nothing less will satisfy him. And just as he likes to appear on good days as the sun coming over the equator; when he has paled in his own estimate he sees himself shunned, interpreting a preoccupied expression as a cut direct.

I cannot describe what Harry has put me through in his tragic moments; and when I am limp and discouraged after the barrage, unable to work and with no heart to play, a telephone call from anyone sly enough to drop in a compliment is sufficient to send him out, treading on air, gullible fool that he is.

If my wife dies before me, Harry has a plan which, he implies, will settle the future for both of us. I must leave the world and save my soul by taking Holy Orders. The change will give me occupation, freedom from frivolous distractions, the assistance of experts in spiritual exercises, relief from money and business cares, and an opportunity to discover my identity.

"And you," I said. "What arrangements have you made for yourself?"

"One thing at a time," he replied. "I've been giving a good deal of thought to the question of how the news is to be broken to the world. It will cause astonishment."

"Won't it be sufficient if I write to my friends? I haven't got so many."

But Harry wasn't satisfied. If I were contemplating such a dramatic step I would do well to anticipate it by telling everyone I met about my resolve, asking them to promise not to breathe it to a soul.

"Cynical behaviour for a budding priest!"

Harry was too preoccupied to answer. This irked me. "May I enquire what you will be doing when I'm giving my impersonation of the Ancient Mariner?" (Harry it was who taught me to introduce literary allusions, at any opportunity, even at the risk of obscuring my meaning.) "Oh," he said, with that simulated diffidence I have good reason to suspect, "I shall need all the time to make out the list of guests for the Ordination ceremony. That will be your last chance to make a splash. We needn't think about your funeral."

FAIR EXCHANGE

I was thrown completely when the first remark he made after we had settled down at our table was, "How's your father?"

"So far as I know, he's all right," I said.

It was too much to hope that Mr Seaver would have brought up the subject of my novel first thing; and I suppose he mentioned my father as a substitute for the weather when he was at a loss for something to say. Both, as it happened, were coming from America at that moment—'a depression is moving eastwards over the Atlantic'. He couldn't have chosen any topic better calculated to crush the euphoria he had aroused by his invitation. Not taking the hint from my manner that the topic was inappropriate at the moment, he went in even deeper.

"I haven't met him for quite a long time. Please tell him when you see him that I was asking for him."

"I will do that," I said in a voice that I hoped would dispose of my father until after lunch.

The restaurant was crowded. I recognised Hilda Farebrother at a table quite close to us; she looked older than the photograph on the dust-jackets of her novels. There was a man with her who looked as if he would slip down her throat at any moment. It might be her publisher. Somehow, seeing them restored my high spirits. I was with a publisher too. It was like a dream; yesterday it would have been a dream, but a telephone call made it real.

To be strictly truthful, in daylight Mr Seaver did not radiate so much charm as he seemed to when we met at a crowded party in Cheyne Walk. He introduced himself on that occasion—out of the corner of my eye I saw him inspecting me out of the corner of his—and I was under his spell at once. Ideas for books went floating up like bubbles in the air; crowns dropped from his pocket; under the chandelier his bald head was bright gold. I had come to think of writing as struggle and rejection, but he dealt only in fame and success; there was no room in his magic cave for other commodities; all I had to do was grasp one of the ideas that he was sending up, let him encapsule it in a contract, whence it would emerge like a butterfly from its chrysalis in much the same manner and rather less time.

The idea that attracted him most and for which I had to feign a sudden enthusiasm was a re-writing of the New Testament something after the plan of Durrell's *Alexandria Quartet*. So much was missing from the gospels; marvellous though they were, they were inadequate in the light of modern psychology. There were hints, but they needed to be followed up. It was mortifying to discover how sketchy my knowledge of the good book was. I had to walk very warily because Mr Seaver had done his homework thoroughly and was full of the subject. Fortunately, he was one of those confiding talkers who make you feel you are contributing to the conversation when all you do is keep your eyes on his face as if it were a camera and make listening noises at frequent intervals. He had all the information.

I would have much preferred to discuss my novel with him. When I mentioned it he looked pleased, but he didn't ask for details, which was rather disappointing. As he was so taken up with this gospel idea, I decided that it would be more tactful to act on his suggestion; when I had finished the book he asked for, then would be the moment to produce the novel. And the delay might be to its advantage. I could look it over. Written in a white heat after the Sylvia disaster, it might be improved by judicious cutting. I'm afraid I put the boot in rather. I was feeling bitter.

"You must come and have lunch with me one day in my office," he said. "There is so much to talk about."

A woman with a hard mouth had been signalling to him
—I hoped he hadn't seen her—he left me to join her. "I'll
get in touch," were his last words.

He didn't.

A month had passed since I floated home from that party
and was afraid to go out again for fear that the telephone
might ring in my absence. I came close to despair. For, in
the meanwhile, the novel came back from yet another publisher with a printed rejection slip and my name mis-spelt on
the label. I began to ask myself if that meeting with Seaver
had been a dream. I dream a lot; and sometimes am not
quite sure whether what is in my mind belongs to my waking
or my sleeping world. They merge in places. But that was
real, and I knew for certain when a secretary rang up and
asked me if I could lunch with Mr Seaver on the following
day at the Swastika.

And I was there, and he was across the table, looking
round the restaurant rather suspiciously, as if he was con-
sidering whether the clientele justified the charges. He gave
a short bow in the direction of some tables, but when his gaze
fell on Miss Farebrother his personality underwent a sudden
change. He put on a playful, naughty expression. It didn't
suit him, and it must have been embarrassing for her because
he chose a moment when she had a too large or too hot piece
of something in her mouth. When she got it down, she tried
to smile at Seaver, and then she said something to the man
with her. I thought his back looked angry.

To bring Seaver's attention round to me, I said, "Isn't
that Hilda Farebrother?" As soon as the words left my
mouth I realised it would have been better to have said, "I
see Hilda Farebrother". I put it in the form of a question
because "That is Hilda Farebrother" would have sounded
silly when he was making those faces at her.

"She's lunching with MacQueen. I pull her leg about it.
He can't let her out of his sight. People think they are lovers,
but the truth is he lives in mortal terror that she may leave

his firm. She's the only name left in their list. I can't read her any more, I find. Can you?"

I didn't know what to say to that. I admire her novels more than anyone's; and if an influence can be detected in my own it is hers. But it didn't seem the moment to start an argument with Mr Seaver and I muttered something about her having written herself out. It was exhilarating to be cutting her up with the most go-ahead publisher in the country; afterwards I would feel ashamed.

Mr Seaver swallowed a whole piece of toast with pâté on it in a gulp.

"Exactly, I told her as much. If I were your publisher, I said, I'd give you £10,000 and tell you to go away—anywhere—and not come back until every penny was spent. Then you would sit down and write a masterpiece. I always speak my mind. I won't kowtow to anyone. Look at MacQueen—I ask you—eating out of her hand. It makes me despair of my profession."

I looked, and I must confess the unworthy thought came into my mind that if Mr Seaver didn't like my novel I might try it on MacQueen. I had no idea he was in such a bad way. MacQueen and Knight were famous publishers when Dickens was in his pram. I was growing very fast. When Seaver talked so lightly about giving all that money away I felt my confidence coming back. Now, at last, this was the man I met at the party. I was glad that I hadn't started up an argument about Hilda Farebrother. If he didn't like her recent novels, it would have been fatal to suggest mine followed roughly the same plan.

"Is your smoked salmon all right?"

The question showed that I had eaten nothing and he had finished his first course. "It's fine," I said, and gobbled up.

Then the next course arrived, and Mr Seaver dug himself in at once. He had a way of worrying it that didn't strike me as attractive. For no reason at all, unless it was because I had been thinking of Sylvia just then, it struck me that Mr Seaver wouldn't be pleasant in bed.

I was thinking of Sylvia because I was thinking of my novel; the two are inseparable. We were half-way through lunch already and nothing had been said about it. Was he waiting for me to introduce the subject? I had the manuscript with me. It seemed absurd to throw away an opportunity to put it into his hands. Not, of course, at the table, but when we were leaving. I had had a brush with the waiter who tried to take it away from me. Seaver saw us: he gave a sharp glance at the parcel; but he didn't say anything, and I thought that perhaps then wasn't the moment to bring up the subject.

Something told me he had forgotten the gospel idea; if that were on he would have got in touch sooner. He couldn't have held off for all this time. If I was wrong I would know very soon, and in that event, I would hold the novel back. That might impress him, because he knew very well what was in the parcel. I know that look.

"You live with your parents?"

The question was so futile, I found it hard to answer civilly.

"Not for years. I've a flat in Egerton Gardens. Rather dreary; but there is room for my books, which is something."

I was trying to get the conversation back on the rails. I even looked across at Miss Farebrother's table, as a gesture of despair.

"I can't remember exactly what it was you said you did."

"I'm writing. I have a job of sorts in the bank. On account of my father. I'm hoping to give it up. He won't like the idea. I don't think anyone could work in a bank and write at the same time, do you? T. S. Eliot couldn't. He gave it up."

"Then you must see quite a lot of your father."

"Not all that much. He's away a great deal for one thing."

Was Mr Seaver regretting the impulse that had led him to invite me out to lunch? The first time we met he had taken me into his world at once; now he seemed determined to keep me bogged down in mine. Was it possible by some hideous coincidence that he had met some other publisher who might have made a disparaging reference to my novel? It's a pretty closed circuit, the book trade, or so I have always heard. They have the same haunts; they talk shop. And my novel had been on the rounds for some time. I could think of no other explanation for his concentration on my boring life. I had to change the subject, and as a compromise I said, "What happened to that gospel idea you were so enthusiastic about?"

Mr Seaver looked puzzled.

"You were discussing the possibility of making the New Testament into a novel."

"Ah! That. I mentioned it to Julia Tottenham and she grabbed at the idea. She has finished Abraham Lincoln, and she was on the look-out for something. This is very much up her street. Her husband had a lectureship in Israel. It's amusing that you should bring up the subject because I must confess to you when we met that evening—where was it?"

"The Leeson Parkes'."

"I remember. I thought you were Julia's younger brother. You were the only man wearing tweeds at the party. And you have quite a look of that family, something about the back of your head. When I told her she said it was a miracle because he was having his gall bladder out that day. I wouldn't put it past him though. It takes one all one's time to keep up with the Tottenhams."

So that was where the gospels had gone. There was only the novel now. In a way, I was relieved. People like Julia Tottenham make books like that look easy. But I would have found it a slog. I don't think a creative writer should dissipate himself in these book-making exercises. I'd have done it to impress my father, who wouldn't believe I was a writer until somebody like Seaver was prepared to pay me money. But if I had my way I would much prefer to have him publish the novel. At least, I had cleared the air.

"How did you find out who I was?"

I tried to sound casual, but the question was a loaded one.

The Leeson Parkes know that I have written this novel; Sylvia was very thick with Joan at one time, and the four of us used to go round together. I don't think Joan gossips, not more than most people anyhow. If Seaver asked her who I was she would almost certainly have said I was a writer. She doesn't know any real writers. That would explain why he got in touch. I wonder how much else Joan told him. I don't mind about Sylvia. Everyone knows about that; I only hoped that she didn't give the impression I had been having trouble placing the book. She read it, and was enormously impressed. But, of course, she had the advantage of knowing the background.

Mr Seaver was smiling comfortably to himself. "This will amuse you," he said, and as he said it, I knew it wouldn't.

"I was lunching at the Balfour only last week when I saw someone come in who was the spit and image of you. You know who I mean. I suppose you are tired of being told you are your father's double. I knew then who you were. I didn't get an opportunity to talk to him. I'd have liked to tell him we had made friends."

"If you're a member of the Balfour, you'll see him there at lunch-time most days."

"I'm not, unfortunately."

"You don't miss very much."

"There I can't agree with you. For anyone who wants to keep in touch, there's no club in London to match it at the moment."

"I'm not a club sort of person, I suppose."

"It never does one any harm to be seen in the right places. Your father is on the committee, I believe."

"Wherever my father is, he's put on the committee. It's as natural to him as breathing."

"He's a very distinguished man. We had a very pleasant evening together once, at a dinner in the City. I would have liked to have reminded him of the occasion."

"He has to go to a good many dinners. It's part of the job. He finds it an awful bore."

"Basil Speare invited me to the Balfour. Between ourselves, I think he did it to impress me. I had to tell him who your father was. He didn't seem to know anyone. Can *you* explain Basil Speare's success? Two years ago he was in Canada, and nobody had ever heard of him. And now I can't pick up a paper without seeing Basil on theatre, Basil on country houses, Basil on oriental art. There must be some reason for it."

Basil Speare was an oracle to me. I would have been very thrilled to meet him. But once again I was being flattered with an opportunity to run someone down. Not to do so was to fall in Mr Seaver's estimation. This time I stalled.

"I know very little about him," I said.

"But can you inform me how, when there's a waiting list a mile long—or so I've been told—for the Balfour, Basil saunters in as if he was raised on the premises? You never heard your father talk about him by any chance?"

"Father has probably never heard of him. He's curiously innocent in these matters. Anything he knows about life he picks up in the *Financial Times*."

"But, dammit, Basil is reviewing science fiction for the *Financial Times*."

"I should think Father skips that item."

"I dare say he does. I don't want to give you the impression that I don't like Basil. We are very good friends, and I think he's going to do a book for me. His push intrigues me: that's all."

Mr Seaver looked quite worked up, and I was beginning to feel utterly depressed. We seemed to be going off at such unpromising tangents. I noticed that success seemed to impress my host; his attitude to my father, for instance; and then, although he seemed to resent Basil Speare's career, yet he lunched with him and was obviously anxious to get him to write. It shows to what I was reduced that I played with the idea of letting him know that I was a member of the Balfour. Quite honestly, it meant nothing to me; I had never darkened its doors since the day my father read me a lecture for appearing in the bar without a tie. But if Mr Seaver set such store by it, would he be impressed if I invited him to lunch there with me? Or would he think it was cheek? He was so bitter about Basil Speare (who is on television once a week at least) getting in that he might be soured beyond recall if he heard that someone who had done nothing yet was able to become a member. I decided to keep my mouth shut.

I went on another tack. I saw that he was fond of his food—he had made an infernal business about ordering the meal—so far I hadn't taken much notice; so I said something complimentary about the wine. He pretended it was beneath my notice; but I had watched him ordering it. I could see that pleased him. I would have to keep on like this. He had recovered his temper again. He was mellowing. Was it possible that he always put on an act like this to impress his authors, to show who was the boss, before he came down to business? Underneath, I could see that he wasn't as confident as I would have expected. I suppose that is because he got to the top of the tree so quickly, and beginning from scratch.

The table was cleared. The coffee was on its away. He had ordered brandy. If anything was going to happen it would happen now. I could feel the maunscript nudging my knee. Mr Seaver offered me a cigar, which I refused, and took some time selecting one for himself. When he got it going, he put his elbows on the table, and brought his face closer to mine. There is a great deal of Mr Seaver when he is not standing up, and it required the whole expanse of uncluttered table cloth to accommodate his expansion. His bulk was a wall between me and the world, but, even without that, I was magnetised by his massive attention. He was concentrating it all on me. I cannot describe the sense of release and fulfilment this transformation in his manner brought to me.

"Tell me," he said, "all about yourself."

I was aware only of his eyes. They got angry very easily,

I had had occasion to observe, but now they were warm and bright and rather moist. In their glow, I fairly melted.

I suppose it was the accumulated effect of those rejections and then the hope on the horizon when I first met Mr Seaver and then the relapse when he seemed to have forgotten me and then the excitement of the telephone call and the growing feeling all through lunch that I was going to be disappointed again—I suppose it had made me unusually susceptible to kindness. At any time I respond when I meet sympathy. And you mustn't forget that there was much more invested in my novel than my ambition to write a book which someone would publish. Perhaps I hadn't allowed enough for the amount of feeling that had gone into it. That could account for the extent to which I let go when Mr Seaver opened the hatches at last.

It was all about Sylvia really. I brought Joe in and called him Marlowe; but even that didn't seem to make him come alive. It was a weakness in the story that I hadn't been able to account for the fascination he had for Sylvia and for so many other girls as well. I intended him to be a foil to the principal character whom I tried not to make too much like myself. But for anyone who knew us, the novel was all about Sylvia and me.

It ended with an orgy, better, I think, than any of those crowd effects Hilda Farebrother attempts as a climax to her novels. I left Sylvia out of it. I was feeling so bitter at the time that I meant to show she was only a small part of a total sexual experience. It was a rather mean revenge. She hated to be left out of anything.

I thought it might be as well when I had this opportunity of telling Mr Seaver about the background of the novel and what happened between Sylvia and me (and the ambivalent part Joe—Marlowe—who was supposed to be my friend played in it) to offer—if he thought it would strengthen the plot—to let Sylvia take part in the orgy. It would mean re-writing the last chapter, but I wouldn't mind doing that if it improved the book as a whole.

I must have gone on for well over half an hour. Never, even when things were going well, had Sylvia given me such rapt attention (she was inclined to interrupt when she suspected references to herself). I had never talked so freely to anyone. I told Mr Seaver about the final break-up with Sylvia, and I tested him out with her theory that by letting Joe have her she was enriching herself and depriving me of nothing. We were all loving friends, she insisted. But when I picked up with Joan she said—which was perfectly true—that I had only done it for revenge. (In the novel I made Joe—Marlowe—get off with Joan, but that didn't happen. He is still with Sylvia.)

Mr Seaver didn't commit himself when I asked these questions. He said he would need to know the people concerned to have an opinion that was of any value.

There was only one couple left in the restaurant by the time I had finished, and the waiters were conveying in sign language that they would like us to go away. I thought Seaver would now leave. I couldn't think what more he could expect me to say. He had taken a sizeable chunk out of his afternoon as it was; and the waiters were making me feel embarrassed. Besides, now that I had been given the opportunity to launch the novel, as it were, I had a childish eagerness to put the manuscript in his hands. I had placed it on the table when I was explaining the plot. It was a marvellous feeling.

"I've been talking far too much," I said. I was feeling emptied out, limp in fact, but quietly happy.

"I was most interested," Mr Seaver said. "You were very good to take me into your confidence. We all have to go through it at one time or another. And I dare say this won't be the last time for you. But you will have learned something from the experience. Life gives us a very sound but a very expensive education."

I was grateful to Mr Seaver, not only because he had been so encouraging; but for listening to what I suppose was a familiar experience. If he thought that, he didn't say so in a hurtful manner. I made up my mind that I would contradict in future the stories that flew around about his ruthlessness and snobbishness. No man of his age had ever been kinder to me.

"Writing it down," he began—I was staggered to hear him going on about the novel. I had expected him to take it and, most likely, send it to the firm's reader—"Writing it down is a useful form of therapy even if it doesn't add up to a saleable book. In this respect women seem to have the edge on men. Several of my friends have been unpleasantly surprised to read what they thought was their secret in an American magazine. When they complain to me, I say: keep away from novelists, not that I have even taken my own advice. One never does, that's why so much advice is given away free. I make a point of paying when I require it. I forget now what I was saying . . . Ah yes, about your novel. I enjoyed our talk; I hope it will be the first of many; where do you lunch as a rule?"

"There's a glorified canteen in the bank."

"Of course. Restaurants are ruinous; I thought your father might take you to his club. I expect he does occasionally."

"Not for years."

"That surprises me. I won't turn your head when I say that if you were my son I'd be glad to show you off. You can tell him that from me. The Balfour is only three blocks away from my office. It would be pleasant if we could meet there occasionally, without any formality. That's what I like about a club. I don't know what has happened to the Jermyn since I became a member—there's never anyone there now. I've given up going; there used always to be someone worth talking to in the bar when I dropped in."

I had been rather hoping he would bring up the idea of lunching in his office. I had been looking forward to that. Perhaps he thought it was too humdrum. Because of my father—I wanted to tell him—he seemed to have quite a false impression of me. I hate formality and fuss of any kind really.

Mr Seaver seemed to be thinking aloud : "If I had an opportunity to talk to your father, I might be able to act as a catalyst. He probably regards your literary interests as a waste of time and connects them in his mind with your girl-friends. I take the view that it is good for a young man to spread himself a bit before he settles down. I know that a shirker will take to the arts as a soft option. But I'm sure you've never refused to roll your sleeves up when the occasion required it."

"I don't mind work provided I believe in what I'm doing."

"I like to hear that."

'Do you think I should tell Father I won't work in his bloody bank any more?"

"I'd be slow to advise you to take such a drastic step as that."

"Better to wait until I'd proved myself."

"Far better."

"I suppose it doesn't matter so long as I know I won't be stuck in the bank for always. T. S. Eliot began life in a bank after all" (I can never think of anyone else who did).

"T. S. Eliot was an exception."

"Yes, of course. I mentioned him only as an example."

We seemed to be at a dead end; but still Mr Seaver showed no disposition to move. The other couple were leaving now. Rather loud, business types, they sounded more friendly than anyone could be this side of Paradise. One of them recognised my host.

"Maurice! How nice to see you," he said, and put a hand on Mr Seaver's shoulder. I noticed the hand; it had a very expensive appearance.

"How are you, my dear?" Mr Seaver said, not appreciat-ing the hand.

Furious with the interruption at that moment, when I was just on the point of handing Mr Seaver the novel, I didn't listen to the falsely hearty exchange. One of them said something about Basil Speare, which I didn't catch, and they all laughed. It was apparently the latest story about the progress of his fiery chariot. If he had come in just then they'd have been all over him, you may be sure.

When they went away eventually, Mr Seaver apologised for not having introduced me.

"Howard is not a bad fellow really, he was laughing at Basil Speare; but there's nobody in our business who is such a climber as himself. When George Crosby got his knighthood, I thought for a time that Howard would go off his head. He went round telling everyone it was a case of mistaken identity. The letter from the Palace was intended for him. Poor Howard."

Only then did I realise that the man we were talking about was Howard Humphrey, the publisher. He is a friend of my father's, a business friend. I have good reason to remember, because when I started to show an interest in writing my father told me that I was on no account to submit anything to that firm. It would look too much like blackmail. Only my father could have thought of such a thing. He is the sort of person that leaves money beside the telephone when he uses it in someone else's house. If Father had known anything about books he would have realised that Howard Humphrey's is the last imprint I'd ever have wanted to come out under. They are very much in the coffee-table side of the business.

My mother who, having nothing else to occupy her, lets cats out of the bag sometimes, told me some time ago that Father was in a sweat because Howard had asked him point-blank to put him up for the Balfour. As always, Father kicked to touch; he's a master of evasive action—has to be in his business; but Howard put him on the spot by blurting out something about his being a Jew, and was that what was worrying Father. After that, of course, there was nothing for it, Father talked to Gordon Grant, and they fixed it between them.

I shouldn't have repeated this, I know; it was letting the old man down rather. I wasn't supposed to know. But I was so close to my goal, and there was so much at stake, I'd have done almost anything at that moment to get my shot in. I found myself retailing that piece of boring gossip about the club just to play Seaver along. He did encourage one to disparage people.

But as soon as I began I felt uncomfortable. Mr Seaver gave me his full attention but not this time with moist eyes. I had that mortifying feeling I was set on the wrong course, that I oughtn't to have begun, but I didn't know how to stop. It was like making a statement to a police officer.

When I had finished rather lamely he said nothing for what seemed a long time. He was thinking. Our waiter, who had been hovering round us miserably, saw his opportunity and swooped down. Mr Seaver ignored him. I had taken up the manuscript before I began my spiel, and I felt foolish clutching it, waiting for Seaver to say something.

The waiter, his nerve broken, had gone back to the corner, and glared at us from there. He had left the bill aeons ago, folded on its plate, in front of Mr Seaver. It must have been very cold by now.

Mr Seaver, very deliberately, took a pair of huge horn-rimmed spectacles out of a case, polished them slowly, and put them on. Then he took up the bill and unfolded it in the same ponderous way. Time passed. It was like waiting for the verdict in a murder trial.

Mr Seaver put the bill down again, took out his pocket book, and paid out the notes, slowly, one by one, until they made a neat pile on the plate.

AT MRS PRESTON'S

HE STOOD LOOKING at the house from the far
side of the road as if he was afraid to come closer; and
indeed, he expected at any moment to see Colonel Plumer's
purple face glaring at him from the window of the sitting-
room or from his bedroom immediately above it. In Mrs
Preston's time the plaster was peeling off the façade, and
the woodwork was thirsting for paint. Now there was an
air of spruceness about the house which extended to its
neighbours. They had all come up in the world. Laurence
noticed three smart plates with bells to match beside the
hall door. The house had been divided into flats.

Laurence Lamb had been the first of Mrs Preston's
boarders, or paying guests as she preferred to call them.
When her husband died at an advanced age she found it
impossible to keep up the large, draughty house in Monkstown on her income, and Laurence's parents, who were
moving to Cork, suggested that she should take their son
in while he worked for his law degree at Trinity College.
This was a friendly arrangement, agreeable to all parties.
The Lambs were glad to think of their first-born under a
watchful eye : Mrs Preston's social position in the terrace
was not threatened by the innovation. But the two guineas
a week paid for Laurence were not sufficient to repair the
deficiency in Mrs Preston's income, even if it had not been
assumed by the Lambs that they were under no rent obliga-
tion during the vacations.

There would have to be other guests. It was a pity, but
then, as one of her friends said, "What are all those empty
rooms doing?" That question may have heated Mrs Preston's

imagination and enlarged her conception—one must remember, too, that Monkstown is a small suburb in which in those days a great deal of tea was taken, a great deal of bridge played, and Mrs Preston's business was everybody's business. Her friends vied with one another to procure suitable additions to her household. Mrs Pratt was first with Mr Roche, much respected in the mysterious world of insurance and now retired. Mrs Adcock said she sent Mr Blenkinsop who lectured in the Veterinary College. Mrs Lyburn was responsible for Arthur Atkinson. He had recently quitted the monastery to study art. A triumph of diplomacy this, because Mrs Preston had been adamant that she would not lower the character of her establishment by taking in students. Larkie Lamb, as a friend, was a special case. Young Mr Atkinson's decorative appearance made him another.

Colonel Plumer must have introduced himself. A widower with a dissolute son in East Africa, his coming was a field-day for Mrs Preston, and left one room only unoccupied. Having gone so far, Mrs Preston was fired to deal herself a full house, but for some reason the inward flow was arrested at this point. Father Murphy, Dr Groves, Mrs Lefanu, Madeleine McGrath, Mrs Potter—none of her friends, rack their brains as they might (and did) could find a suitable candidate. Colonel Plumer may have put them off. With the exception of Laurence, the cut of whose jib he approved of, he refused to be civil to the other guests. In a way they respected him for it.

Mr Blenkinsop put forward a relative, Miss Alice Spring, serious and elderly, as a possible solution, for which he got no thanks. In general, Mrs Preston decided it would be better not to have—as she put it—'too many women around the place'. The idea of a childless couple—Germans, also friends of Mr Blenkinsop—seemed obscurely indecent when he suggested it. She couldn't have said why. "I wouldn't like the thought of it, somehow, would you?" she said to Mrs Potter. "I know what you mean," Mrs Potter replied delicately. It might have brought an unsettling element into a celibate atmosphere. Curiously, this did not occur to Father Murphy, but then, he was beginning to tire of the minutiae of Mrs Preston's arrangements. He had troubles of his own. To advertise in the newspaper as he suggested would have been a betrayal of the spirit of the enterprise and reduce what had at best a tenuous resemblance to a prolonged house-party to the sordid reality of a common lodging-house.

Such was the state of the case when Mr Edwards made his appearance. After forty years Laurence relived the scene. The household assembled as usual for high tea at six o'clock ('I can't afford to give them dinner') when, without any warning, Mrs Preston appeared with a bald man and said, "I want you all to meet Mr Edwards." They knew at a glance that Mr Edwards wouldn't do. Not because he looked like a beetle : Mr Blenkinsop resembled a newt, and age and anaemia had left little of Mr Roche to admire. It was not a mere question of personableness; Mr Edwards's aura made a mockery of the principles upon which Mrs Preston had built up her establishment. And it was very soon made apparent to all that Mrs Preston was more fully aware of his unsuitability than any of her guests.

As she went round the table giving their names, each saw the repudiation in her eye. Only Colonel Plumer gave expression to his own disapproval. He looked for a moment as if he was about to have a seizure; then he said, "When are we going to begin? This is the second day that the meal has not been on time." He was the only one ever to complain to Mrs Preston to her face. On this occasion she seemed to welcome the diversion.

Mr Edwards was on the wrong side of forty and he spoke with the accent of the English Midlands. Mrs Preston made it obvious that she had thrown him to the lions when she neither invited him to sit beside her nor even asked anyone to make room for him. He had to stand there like a malefactor in the pillory; but the smile that he was wearing when he came in never left his face. "That's very kind," he said when Laurence moved away from Atkinson and left space for a chair between them. Smiling, he asked each youth in turn what he did, and only interrupted once, to ask for tomato ketchup.

"There isn't any, I'm afraid," Mrs Preston said, turning for support to Colonel Plumer. He reared his head and seemed to bay.

"My husband used to say that you could know the difference between a three-star hotel and a no-star hotel at a glance. The no-star hotel always had three bottles of commercial travellers' sauce on every table."

Mrs Preston was addressing the company, apparently; but as the anecdote drew to a close she looked round for a face to leave it with. It was a way she had when using the late Preston as a flail. On this occasion she chose the Colonel's. Mr Blenkinsop wasn't paying attention; the young men did not look as if they wanted to be drawn into an attack on the newcomer, even though he was boring them with his polite attentions. And Mr Roche for once seemed unwilling to be addressed as confidant-in-chief and adviser-general. The late Mr Preston was disinterred whenever his widow felt the need for a potent ally. Laurence Lamb was the only guest who had had the privilege of his acquaintance. An elderly retired Corporation official, he had lived like a moth in his wife's buoyant upholstery. It was extraordinary to see the use to which he could now be put, serving the purpose of the man's hat and stick lone ladies left on show in the hall, hoping to frighten off burglars.

The Colonel's teeth and a slice of bacon were fighting an unequal battle at that moment, and except to show veins in his forehead, he was unable to bring up reinforcements. Mr Edwards continued to smile.

Mrs Preston's antipathy to her new boarder made it reasonable to suppose that she would take someone into her confidence and explain how he managed to get in. She put all the blame on Mrs Potter. That lady had called at lunchtime with the air of Florence Nightingale disembarking at

Scutari. She had solved Mrs Preston's problem. This rich
and delightful Englishman was looking out for a suitable
flat and was staying meanwhile at the Shelbourne Hotel.
Mrs Potter had used her powers of persuasion, and with a
daring that surprised herself had proposed his coming to Mrs
Preston and paying five guineas a week. He hadn't hesitated,
and said that if Mrs Potter recommended Mrs Preston that
was enough for him. He was prepared to move in without
even asking to examine the premises.

Mrs Preston considered her friend in many ways a fool.
Where men were concerned she was as silly as a schoolgirl,
and Mr Potter's patience was proverbial. But in the present
instance his handsome offer to pay twice the going rate
recommended Mr Edwards to her. That he represented a
mammoth mustard manufacturer did not tell in his favour;
but she had no experience of the business world to guide her.
She could not rule out a businessman as such. It was too
arbitrary. One must move with the times.

Mr Edwards arrived as high tea was on its upward jour-
ney, and Mrs Preston had not recovered from the shock of
his epiphany when she introduced her most recent acquisi-
tion to the rest of her collection.

"I will never speak to Pansy Potter again," she told
Laurence later, and, no doubt, Colonel Plumer. Pride prevented her from opening her soul to the rest of the household, but she made her attitude sufficiently clear. If Mr
Edwards chose to stay he must expect no quarter. That was
all she had to say. He either failed to notice the direction
of her barbs, or his skin was actually as thick as it looked,
or he gave Mrs Preston the licence an explorer would con-
cede to aborigines among whom he settled for purposes of
scientific observation. He was complacent and condescending
but unrelentingly kind.

"Coming for a feed?" he said to Colonel Plumer when
the latter pretended not to recognise him on the footpath
outside the Salthill Hotel. The Colonel was doing no such
thing; and he impressed the fact so emphatically on Mr

Edwards that he never addressed a word to that officer again, while never ceasing to maintain that he was 'a great old boy'. Of Mrs Preston his only complaint was the iron quality of her rations. "Coming for a feed?" he said to Laurence; and when they were seated at the table he expatiated on the topic. "Seeing as how she charges five guineas a week, I think we are entitled to expect better," he said. Laurence did not correct this statement, but he had no wish to be drawn into a conspiracy with Mr Edwards against Mrs Preston.

"The bread is always stale. Have you noticed, Larkie? It's my belief she buys it a day old. Gets it cheap that way."

Mr Edwards did himself no good talking like this to any of the household. Whatever they might suffer from Mrs Preston individually, they would close ranks against Mr Edwards. Neither did Laurence like to be called 'Larkie' by Mr Edwards, and he deprecated the importance Mr Edwards attached to food and the way he said the waitress had a nice little bum.

It was only a matter of time before he would be given his marching orders—that was the general opinion—if he was not frozen out beforehand.

But if that was the impression he made in Mrs Preston's establishment, there were incontestable proofs that Mr Edwards was in demand elsewhere. Whenever the telephone rang, the betting was even money that the call was for him. And it did not pass unnoticed that the voice on the line was invariably a woman's, sometimes a very fetching voice. It was soon common knowledge that the mantelpiece in Mr Edwards's room was thick with invitation cards. He was busy with a tailor, from whom boxes arrived by special delivery. Seemingly unaware of disapproval, he asked for the general opinion about his choice of material and the cut.

"I'm very particular about hand-stitching," he said. "How does it look at the back?"

This gave opportunities for ribaldry of which only Mrs Preston ever took advantage. The lodgers were a mild-spoken lot, the Colonel excepted, but he kept himself out of Mr Edwards's way, and the latter, trusting as he was in general, was careful not to invite comments when the old soldier was anywhere in the vicinity.

Mrs Preston had her own apartments; access to them was governed by a hierarchical rule and was the ultimate test of a guest's standing. The Colonel could come in whenever he cared to (since Mr Edwards's advent he practically lived in Mrs Preston's sitting-room). She liked a man about the place just as much as she disapproved of too many women (by which she meant more than one), and when her friends came to call she was by no means averse to their finding the Colonel in the best armchair. Laurence Lamb, the youngest in the house, but the first to come and the only one with legitimate claims to friendship—the only genuine hall-marked 'guest'—had also the right to come and go when he pleased. But the Colonel's oppressive presence kept Laurence out, and he preferred the younger company of Arthur Atkinson. Mr Roche came in when invited; that is to say whenever Mrs Preston needed his advice. The others were sometimes called in to make numbers up when Mrs Preston entertained. Mr Edwards was in this respect unique; since the day he arrived he was never allowed to come into the sanctum. Five guineas a week entitled him to bed and board; for half that amount all the other guests were entitled as well to rationed shares of Mrs Preston's personal friendship.

Laurence, coming in early one afternoon, was captured by Mrs Preston in the hall. She was in a considerable state of agitation, and begged him to come to her room and have a word with her. The remains of afternoon tea were on view, and Mrs Preston told Laurence to help himself. Which he did. The fare in the inner apartment was of a higher standard than the guests were accustomed to.

"I can talk to you as a friend, Larkie. I can't tell you what a relief that is. Have you heard the latest?"

Laurence, his mouth full of cream cake, was unable to answer, but he swallowed hugely and shook his head.

"Take as many of those as you like," she said. "They won't keep. Pansy Potter has invited the Edwards man to her party. She broke the news to me today. 'I hope you don't mind,' she said. I wasn't going to let her get away with that. 'I mind very much, I don't mind telling you,' I said. 'I think the least you should have done was to ask me before you took such a step. It places me in a very humiliating position. I cannot understand you, Pansy,' I said. 'You imposed this creature on me in the first place and against my better judgement. I knew that you had done so in an effort to help me. God knows, I needed the money. Clement would turn in his grave if he saw what I was reduced to. His abiding fear was that he would not leave me enough to keep up my position. What I still cannot understand is how having met this Edwards person you could have possibly entertained, even for a second, the idea that he would be a suitable addition to my little household. With one eye, across a field in a fog, I could tell you all you wanted to know about Mr Edwards, at a glance.' Of course she had no answer. I wonder was she drunk at the time. And the trouble with Pansy is—don't ever say I said this—anything in trousers goes to her head immediately. Some women are like that. I'm not suggesting anything nasty, mind you. In spite of what she has done to me I'm very fond of Pansy, and Philip is such a fine person. I'm sure he has been very much upset by all this. He wouldn't breathe a word, of course. He knows that Pansy loses her head and makes a fool of herself on occasions. This is not the first time. Not by any means. I shall never forget the Christmas party at Madeleine McGrath's when the Belgian consul made eyes at her. I wept for my sex that night. But that is beside the point. I'm faced now with the prospect of this dinner for Philip's fiftieth birthday. Pansy has been going on about it for weeks. She is enlarging the table so as to sit fourteen. That, I will tell you, was her excuse. She had lost track of her numbers and only yesterday discovered that she was sitting down thirteen to dinner. She panicked then, she pretends, and invited Mr Edwards to make up the even number. 'That is no excuse,' I said; 'and besides I cannot conceive of any bad luck likely to arise from our sitting down thirteen to table that would be worse than the presence of Mr Edwards at the party.' Then she said something to cover herself about there being one woman too many. As much as to suggest that I was the cause of the trouble. 'Why didn't you ask me to drop out,' I said, 'if you were so concerned about even numbers?' You can imagine how she went on then. Without me the party would be nothing. 'You may ask anyone or everyone so far as I am concerned so long as Daisy Preston's there.' That she assured me was all Philip had to say about the evening's entertainment.

"You might as well finish the éclairs. The meringues will do for another day."

Nothing was ever the same after Mrs Potter's party. Mr Edwards saw no reason to disguise the fact that he had been invited; but whenever he referred to it in Mrs Preston's presence she gave him the verbal equivalent of a kidney punch. He was always impervious to her insults, and it was characteristic of what must be seen as the large charity of the man that he took as a matter of course that he should ferry Mrs Preston back and forth in a taxi on the great night. There were those who thought she would refuse; but she took the sensible course and secured free transport at least from the ruin of the evening. The setting forth was watched from several windows. Even Colonel Plumer, who always pretended to be unaware of what was going on, was taking a peep.

The return was heard but not seen. There was a definite passage of time after the hall door opened and before Mr Edwards ascended the stairs. He was humming very softly the overture from *William Tell*.

"How did the party go?" Laurence Lamb asked him at breakfast. Mrs Preston had not come down.

"Oh, very nicely, thank you," Mr Edwards replied.

Nobody dared to open the subject with Mrs Preston, and

she volunteered no information. She had become strangely silent. It was apparent that a momentous change had taken place when Mr Edwards was seen to enter Mrs Preston's drawing-room. Other marks of sudden favour were displayed. He was offered second helpings. He was asked if the soup was flavoured to his liking. The bread at table lost its stale taste. There had been nothing comparable to this since the miracle of the loaves and fishes.

Yet Mr Edwards did not change. He continued to say "Coming for a feed?" to any lodger who happened to fall in his way on Fridays. The telephone continued to ring for his attention; invitations kept pouring in.

But Mrs Preston changed. She had always been ebullient, she was now as unpredictable as the weather. One day she was all mockery and laughter, another she was sad and silent. Her silences were against nature, and strangely oppressive to her guests. Sometimes she was seen to have been crying. She bought herself strange costumes and absurd hats. She frequently lost her temper.

But what was most remarkable was her attitude to the telephone. The idea of Mrs Preston's deigning to answer a bell of any description was unthinkable until she was actually seen doing this. Not only did she rush to the telephone whenever it rang, she called back anyone who attempted to forestall her. And the calls were, of course, more often than not for Mr Edwards.

Mrs Preston and the telephone became a non-stop revue for the entertainment of her lodgers. Her solo performance was watched with amusement at first and, later, dismay. Her telephone manner became terse to the point of rudeness. And sometimes she was rude. Then came the day when Mr Edwards let it be known that he was demanding an explanation why a certain call had not been passed on to him, why Mrs Preston had said he was out on an occasion when he was in. He mentioned these matters factually, without rancour, as he used to criticise the bread.

"This can't go on, you know. It isn't reasonable," was

all he said to Mr Roche and Mr Blenkinsop, the older men. With the young his manner was more fatherly. He inquired about the progress of ther studies. He was first with congratulations always. "Education," he said, "is the thing."

About this time Laurence Lamb heard the results of his law degree examination. He had passed. Mrs Preston gave a little entertainment in his honour. Even Colonel Plumer came. "God bless you, my boy," he said to him. He stank of brandy. Mr Edwards gave Laurence a book in which he had written in a copper-plate hand an affectionate inscription. Shortly after this party, Laurence took a legal post in one of the remaining British colonies. And then war came.

Laurence crossed the road and read the names on the elegant plates : Nuttal—Robinson—Atkinson. *Atkinson*. Was it possible that the pale youth, who kept his monastery's fallen day about him, was living here still! Thirty-eight years had passed since Laurence Lamb came through that door for the last time. It was now a smooth egg-yellow colour; it used to be a sick green.

The temptation to try to get in became irresistible. Laurence pushed the Atkinson bell. The door was opened by an elderly man, spectrally thin, in a gay shirt and rather tight tartan trousers. He stood looking at Laurence nervously, waiting for him to explain himself.

"I used to live in this house. I just happened to be in the neighbourhood and when I saw the name Atkinson I took the liberty of ringing the bell. There used to be—"

Over the nervous face passed a spasm like a smile.

"I thought I recognised you. Laurence Lamb. Won't you come in? My friend is at the supermarket, but he will be back very shortly."

Laurence did not recognise the partitioned hall through which they passed. It brought to mind a horse-box. Neither was the narrow stair familiar; but he knew the room into which he followed the matchstick figure of his former fellow-lodger. The window looked out at what used to be the Salthill Hotel. But now where the building had been was a space surrounded by trees. "This was my room," Laurence said. "But it looked very different then."

There was a chaste elegance and a faintly oriental ambience about the Atkinson furniture and decorations. Japanese prints on the wall set the tone. Chinoiserie was carefully displayed on painted shelves. There was no clutter and no comfort. A child in this room would have been as out of place as a stalled ox.

"This is a very odd coincidence," Atkinson said, "your coming just now. I was only saying to myself the other day that I must find out where you were. I've had a book of yours all these years; I'm so glad of the opportunity to get it off my conscience."

He jumped up boyishly and went to one of his well-ordered shelves. The volume in a red mock-leather cover which he pulled out looked pathetic and shabby in contrast to his own fine bindings—Shakespeare in the cheap Oxford pre-war edition. On the fly-leaf was written :

To Larkie
To celebrate his distinguished degree
(Hons.) from his affectionate friend
W. Edwards
15th October 1938

"I wish my friend were here. I do want you to meet him. Won't you stay to tea?"

Laurence, plunged into the past, felt an unreasonable aversion to Atkinson's friend and to Atkinson for so insensitively living in the present even if it were in the guise of a pressed flower. He had a plane to catch, he said; and Atkinson tiresomely catechised him about the time the plane went, revealing hours of empty afternoon to fill.

"What are you doing nowadays?" he said politely, having given Laurence a fullish picture of his life in the museum.

Laurence, who hadn't been listening, said, "I am longing to know what happened after I left. How extraordinary that you should have stayed on."

"Oh my dear, I didn't *stay on*. It was quite a coincidence. I had been looking everywhere for a flat when my friend— I wonder what's keeping him—said there was one in Monkstown that he had heard about. Well, you can imagine how I felt when I discovered where it was. It has taken me ten years to create my own atmosphere.

"Mrs Preston sold the house after the Colonel died. That was a terrible business. He choked over a bone at the table when someone contradicted him. Nobody could be found belonging to him, and if we hadn't all subscribed Mrs Preston would have had to stump up for the funeral. He hadn't paid her a penny for years, it seemed; and he left a huge bill at the grocer's too. Drank like a fish, of course. Mrs Preston called me in one day and said she would have to give up. She had a sister living somewhere in Kerry. A rather silent woman with a slight moustache. She used to come and stay in Horse Show week. Mrs Preston went off to live with her. But everything was at sixes and sevens by that time. She never looked up after Mr Edwards went."

"Tell me about that."

"There's not very much to tell really—Oh, I wish my friend were here to meet you—you remember all the trouble there used to be about telephone calls. Mrs Preston became so jealous. One day he accused her in front of us all of intercepting his mail. There was a frightful scene. He left next day. Moved into a hotel, I believe. And then I heard he had gone back to England. It was all so long ago. Do you know, I had almost forgotten his name until I thought of it just now."

"And how did Mrs Preston get on down in Kerry?"

"Very well. Quite recovered her spirits. Took to golf, and beat all-comers, if her account is to be believed."

"She was a great old sport."

"And very fond of you. We called you the star boarder.

Did you know that? She often mentions your name. I don't suppose you would have time to call and see her."

"Mrs Preston's alive! But she must be a hundred."

"Not quite. She's very deaf, poor dear, but otherwise remarkably well. Her sister left her quite comfortably off. She stays in a hospice run by nuns. It's quite near. I'll write down the address."

The prospect of meeting Mrs Preston again made Laurence impatient; Atkinson's insistence that St Catherine's Bower was within a few minutes' walk did not reconcile him to any lingering here, waiting for the missing friend. Atkinson had never been more than a rather ineffectual spear-carrier in the drama which was enacted under Mrs Preston's roof. He insisted on talking about his life in Monkstown, refusing to accept his rôle as a *revenant*.

When Laurence was trying to calculate Mrs Preston's age, Atkinson said it was not until one saw one's contemporaries that one realised how old one was getting oneself. The thought had occurred to Laurence, but he derived no satisfaction from hearing it expressed by Atkinson. It was clearly time to go.

"I do wish you'd stay. The Bower is only just around the corner," he said when Laurence refused to be held any longer.

"Do you ever come to England? We would be delighted to see you if you found yourself near Poole." Atkinson said he didn't go to England nowadays. He found it so crowded, but if he had reason to, he would be very glad to avail himself of Laurence's invitation. He didn't ask for a more precise address.

Laurence was foot-sore when he arrived at the Bower, half an hour later. Mrs Preston must be quite comfortably off nowadays, was his reassuring impression when he found himself being escorted to her room by a cheerful nun.

"Here's a young man to see you, Mrs Preston." She shouted so loudly that Laurence thought for a moment the nun had gone mad.

There had always been so much of Mrs Preston—voice, figure, everything in such generous helpings—that it was impossible at first glance to reconcile that overflowing personality with the little face, propped up by pillows, that stared at Laurence from the clean white bed. She concentrated eyes as bright as a bird's on her visitor while the nun endeavoured to explain who he was, trying her voice at various pitches, then at last writing 'Mr Lamb' on a piece of paper.

"Can't shee, no shpectacles," Mrs Preston said cheerfully. But she never took her eyes off the man in the room nor stopped smiling. Laurence was glad he came.

The nun made a supreme effort. Making a megaphone of her hands, she pronounced L A M B very distinctly, and then pointed at Laurence to avoid a misunderstanding.

As a balloon is gradually inflated, recognition dawned on Mrs Preston's face, then—as it were—burst.

"Larkie," she said as delightedly as absence of teeth allowed, and looked from one to the other to distribute her pleasure in fair shares. She held out a little hand to Laurence, and grasped his and held it in a tight warm grip like a baby's.

"I'll leave you two together," the nun said.

After that there was nothing in the reunion to reassemble in words. He did a lot of shouting; she nodded and smiled. It was exhausting for Laurence. But the old lady was thriving on it. "More, more, more," she seemed to be saying. A clock beside the bed warned him that there was very little left of what from the other end looked like a long afternoon.

She saw the direction of his glance. The happy look left her face. She stared at him, not reprovingly, but as if she wanted to tell him something and could not remember what it was. And then, with an anxious glance at the door, she signalled to him to give her a japanned box that lay on a table out of reach.

Still watching the door suspiciously, she searched under her pillow for her handbag, extracted a key and opened the box. She looked exactly like a bird as she rummaged in this. Then she gave a little sigh of pleased relief.

As one who handled holy things, she put a small folder into Laurence's hand.

When he looked at her face for a cue, she became impatient. 'Open it, can't you' she seemed to say. And she smiled 'That's more like it' when he took out the snapshots that the folder contained.

They were not very clear or in perfect focus—views of what looked like public gardens. In the foreground of each a fat man stood, sheltering his eyes from the sun. In one snap taken beside a municipal pond, his stance was curiously like the duck's in the same picture. There was the same comfortable sleekness and lack of hurry. Head disproportionately large, legs shorter than Laurence remembered; it could be nobody other than Mr Edwards.

When Laurence mimed his pleasure, exaggerating it for Mrs Preston's benefit, she reached out an eager hand. He returned the photographs, and she looked at each one with the concentration a chimpanzee gives to the inspection of a banana. For a few minutes she forgot Laurence while she relived those enchanted days. How often, he wondered, did she give herself this treat? The secrecy with which the ceremony had been conducted, the air of conspiracy conjured up, suggested that the occasions were rare. She was having an orgy.

Laurence's attention wandered round the room. He was glad to see his old friend was ending her days in cheerful comfort. The window gave out into a pleasant garden. All was as well with her as it could be, and it was time for him to go.

Mrs Preston must have read his thoughts; she put down the photographs. 'Shall I put them back in the box?' he mimed.

She nodded acquiescence. But when he began to put them into their folder, she snatched at one, and beckoned him to study it with her. It showed Mr Edwards sniffing at a large rose in his buttonhole. As she looked at it, she moved her head slowly from side to side as if she was listening to an old tune. Then she looked full into Laurence's face. Her eyes were trying to tell him something; something immeasurably sweet, a secret she had decided, after long hoarding, to share with someone. And she might never see her star boarder again.

"Marvalishkish," she murmured, her eyes lost in dreaming now. "Marvalishkish." He strained to hear what she was trying to say. "Marvalishkish," she repeated, nodding her head to the music of it. But still he couldn't understand. A glance of impatience as at a child whose slowness to learn looks suspiciously like stubbornness made Laurence blush. Reassured, she said—this time more distinctly—M A R V A L I S H K I S H.

Was it something in the way she pointed at the photograph as if in despair at his failure to catch the last message she had to send in this world that enlightened him at last?

"Marvellous kiss." His lips followed hers. She nodded, but gravely now. He shared the responsibility for the secret. She put the snapshots back and locked the box. He returned it to its place on the table. At the door he turned to take his last look at Mrs Preston.

She raised a finger to her lips.

BANG

I LIKE IT when one of my academic friends invites me
to dine in college. Nostalgia, of course, plays its seductive
part; but I am bound to admit that everything looks better
than it did in my time. Government aid wasn't thought of
then, and would have been suspect anyhow for the reason
that we all knew—almost the only tag left to me now—
Timeo Danaos et dona ferentes.

Trinity College, Dublin, with a Chancellor of the Roman
Catholic persuasion. Women at the high table, and Maoists
free to heckle guests uncongenial to the new puritans—these
and other innovations would have been seen—unfairly—as
the strings the Greeks attached to the parcel, and not for
what they are—obedience to the Zeitgeist.

The cellar has been admirably kept up—I never thought
I would find a Sauterne I could drink after dinner at my
time of life—and everywhere there was gloom and grime is
now, literally, as fresh as paint. Was it as elegant as this in
the eighteenth century? My generation inherited from its
Victorian forebears a monstrous theory that old meant dull.
They allowed themselves to be persuaded that the great
paintings of the world had been covered with dark varnish
by the artists; they were horrified at the suggestion that the
Greeks used colour on their statues. Gloom was the symbol
of the highest good, gravity the mark of excellence—a
sepulchral voice was used to practise for a place in the
heavenly choir.

On Friday evening, I half closed my eyes, and saw the
dining-hall lit by candles, lending it a mystery that electric
light has chased away, brilliant with a company in periwigs

and suits of velvet, as richly coloured as the fruit that grows on walls that face the sun. An illusion, of course; there would have been a preponderance of snuff colour, black and drab shades inevitably, save for the academic robes, and these —tonight—are splendid. A prematurely grey doctor of laws with hair *en brosse* might be a contemporary of the younger Melbourne.

We had been talking about changes, not only those for the better—the renovations—but the changing attitudes towards custom and authority. For how much longer would undergraduates endure the protracted ceremony at the conferring of degrees, for instance? "Gimme," they would soon be shouting, and rushing forward to grab their parchments, having better ways of employing their time than sitting listening to long-winded citations. Many of them, my neighbour on the right, a lecturer in botany, assured me, give a reluctant hearing to the customary saying of grace on Commons. All these ceremonies are seen as the trappings of the Great Conspiracy, symbols of a confidence trick perpetuated from time immemorial, whereby the monopoly of power is retained and the fraud gilded over and given divine sanction. The Romans making gods of the emperors led with trumps; the cards have had to be played with more finesse since the barbarians dealt themselves a hand.

Given any encouragement he might have developed his theme, but the political economist on my other side did not conceal his impatience with the prospect and took me over at the first opportunity, resolutely ignoring my sociable efforts to draw him into the conversation. He had his own subject, had lain in wait for an audience, and was not going to share his capture. He was full of a high-level conference under the auspices of the United Nations that he had recently attended.

"I must tell you about a conversation we had at lunch one day during the conference, it was an eye-opener to me. Merely as a diversion, with no intention of starting up a serious discussion, you understand, I made the suggestion that, as private morality had become anarchistic, we needed a code for public morality, a new Decalogue.

"An Indian, who had charmed us all, the most completely civilised of the delegates, I should have said, took up the idea at once. What was to be the first commandment? THOU SHALT NOT HAVE APARTHEID. It was my suggestion, and I could see at once that everyone agreed it had been chosen in its proper place. So much so that I began to think of the set that had been given to Moses. The order there is haphazard. No slackness of that sort would have been allowed here. So much so that it became evident we were going to get up from the table without any other commandments but the one. I was beginning to regret that I had ever ventured on the game when an African delegate spoke non-stop for ten minutes. There was no hope of stemming the flow. I tried to catch the eye of the Indian, who had been discussing Lowell's poetry with me when we came in. But I could not attract his attention. He was listening to the monologue with an attention which was not dictated by politeness. He was absorbed. But I was being bored to tears.

"At last, as a sick joke, and in a desperate effort to rescue the table from a topic introduced as light relief, I asked the Indian if he thought it would be allowable to throw a bomb into a bus-load of white women and children if it were done to further the cause of racial equality. I expected to be called to order at once; and that would have served my purpose. The conversation could have been brought back into some agreeable channel. But, to my astonishment, the Indian gave every indication that he was treating my question with the utmost seriousness. As for the eloquent African, so far from being pulled up by my macabre question, he replied at once that if a well-directed bomb could further the cause, he had no hesitation in saying the more the merrier.

"The Indian, in a more judicial manner—and I found that this was more spine-chilling—agreed that while he was opposed in principle to all violence, including the killing of animals to eat them, nevertheless, if one such act was inspired by a genuine and reasonable belief that it could further this tremendous cause, then he would have to condone it. 'I wouldn't give the person concerned a medal, mark you,' he said with his dazzling smile for my benefit. I was not amused.

"What shocked me was the discovery of such a moral abyss between us, and the realisation that the white man was responsible for digging it. For the rest of the meal I sat in silence while the African and the Indian discussed a question which had spoilt a pleasant occasion for me."

At this point my talkative neighbour remembered his dinner. I had noticed his veal cutlets were looking uncomfortable. Now, belatedly, he set about giving them his undivided attention, having succeeded in his object of rescuing me from the equally talkative botanist on my right. I was left conversationally stranded. There was a time when this would have depressed me, but not now. Nowadays I prefer to listen than to talk and to look than to listen. As I grow older I find that I am relying more and more on my eyes for my entertainment.

I look from one to another of the faces at the long tables and wonder what each mask conceals. Seated in front of me is a shapeless man of indeterminate age with an expressionless face. He is apparently alone, without the responsibilities of a host or the duties of a guest. He has paid for his dinner —or he will pay for it—and he is eating it without enjoyment as he might cut his toenails. He does not look as if he is thinking about anything, and is concentrating on the business of getting his food into his face. His neighbours are ignoring him. I do not have a fellow-feeling for him on this account because I know that very soon my untalked-to condition will be observed and remedied; but he, except for the business of passing salt, has not tried to talk to anyone since dinner began and nobody has talked to him. He is an island in conversational traffic. It is his destiny. There were always some of them on the staff at college. When you heard they were married, it came as a surprise. How was the matter arranged? He seems to ask nothing and to give nothing, to live in a condition of permanent neutrality, in an emotional Switzerland. I see him reading yesterday's newspaper for choice and returning year after year to the same lodgings for the same holiday. He must perform some function. He sets about it as he set about his dinner this evening and proceeds at a pace that makes a mistake almost an impossibility. Now he has finished all before him. He lays down knife and fork and sits staring in front of him at nothing, waiting for the next course.

And then I think about the Indian who had such unbending views about the suppression of apartheid. I can see him and hear him. It is only because his English is too perfect that I know he cannot be English. At Oxford or Cambridge he was the best speaker in the Union. His clothes will be faultlessly cut and, at one time, would have been made only by a London tailor. His hair will be grey and he may be wearing a flower in his lapel. The handkerchief in his pocket is silk, and his shirt is also. He makes his English confrères look and sound as if they had been manufactured from sausage-meat. If he were here he would—unless someone unhappily brought up the subject of apartheid—be talking charmingly, making difficult things easy, everything delightful accessible; and violence, rudeness, obtuseness, awkwardness, ignorance —remote and unthinkable. But he said it could be right to throw a bomb at a bus!

I looked at the face in front of me; it had moved sufficiently to acknowledge the service of the waiter who had removed the plate, and then resumed its wooden impassivity. A hedgehog moves thus when attention is paid to it. I tried to imagine myself, who have never handled any weapon, aiming with a pistol at the centre of that not very white shirt, the third button. I can shoot if I please and when I please. The button will be there. I shall not have to account for my action to anyone here or elsewhere. When I pull the trigger the bullet will pass through the button and the man will be dead. He will continue to stare in front of him. There will still be no expression on his face. I never knew him or talked to him. He was, is, and will be nothing to me. His shirt button on which I am concentrating has more character than himself. It will be the centre of the only exciting thing that ever happened to him. He has never felt anything before. Nothing ever became him as his death. I am giving him his only significant moment. Life in death in exchange for death in life.

In dumb show I hold the silver knife in my right hand steady and feel the trigger. You don't pull the trigger, I was told, you squeeze the trigger.

I don't know how long I sat there afterwards; there was nothing, you must understand, that looked in any way remarkable about the manner in which I held my knife. I looked like any man eating veal. The action had taken place only in my imagination. The man's face did not alter its expression; but the button at which I had taken aim gleamed like a distant star. A trick of the light, perhaps.

There is a fuss at the table. The guests rise. My placid friend takes no notice, and does not move. There is no change in the expression of that imperturbable face. Nothing to show that he is any less alive than he ever was. He must have been heavy. It took three to carry him, and one puffed quite a lot. He was older than the others.

CAESAR'S PLATTER

L I O N E L S P A R R O W , T H E editor of the most liberal
of the national dailies, lived in constant fear of ambush by
cranks. As a species they regarded themselves as having
natural claims upon his time and attention. He developed
self-protective mechanisms, and learnt how to smell a bore
downwind at thirty paces. When Richard Martin cornered
him he was escaping from a tied house, and cursed himself
for not running for cover at once when he saw a stranger
smile at him. Before Martin even identified himself, the editor
knew what was coming and had a refusal ready to deliver.
No. It was not feasible at the moment to publish a series of
articles about the Far East.

Sparrow derived no pleasure from disappointing people.
It made him sad; and he was painfully conscious that sometimes a man of talent was put down where a persistent dud
would have fought his way in. He extricated himself so pain-
lessly on this occasion that he felt at once he must have made
a mistake. These articles were possibly worth attention.
Martin had a small reputation as a novelist, and he had
spent several years in the Far East. He might be worth encouraging. And then the editor remembered. He retraced his
footsteps.

"If you have any time to spare, I heard my deputy saying
that he was looking for someone to interview Howard
Harper. He has bought himself an estate over here to take
advantage of the income tax concessions. His last novel was
set in Vietnam, as, I suppose, you know."

Martin did not know. He had never read a line by Howard
Harper, whom he classed in his mind with detergent powders;

but he had time on his hands and next to nothing in his pocket.

"I could have a try. I'm not an authority on Harper's work. Does that matter?"

"Not in the least. Come back to the office with me now; and we can get you fixed up."

Twenty-four hours later Martin was looking down from the crest of a Wicklow hill upon a Georgian mansion set in a grove of sheltering trees. A river meandered through meadows in which Ayrshire cattle made dappled splotches in a green landscape. Over all, a mountain presided. Not an awesome peak; a mild mountain of the height required to complete the design of the picture.

A crash course in Mr Harper's fiction had not conditioned Martin to reconcile this reward with that contribution to literature. He felt a sudden aversion to the commission he had undertaken. The editor had turned down, without troubling to look at them, informed articles above the standard of what usually appeared in his newspaper, and thrown him this interviewing task as a consolatory bone. Martin had read other accounts of interviews, all written in an adulatory tone; the reporter, as it were, gazing up from below at the hero on a height. He was damned if he would fawn on anyone who used words as if they were sods of turf. But it was easier, having come so far, to go on. How could he explain his change of mind to a busy editor?

He was not in a professional frame of mind when he pulled the bell and waited for—? A footman in livery, an eastern slave, an Irish biddy or the Great Man Himself.

It was the last—there was no doubt about it—who came out to welcome him. A professional middle-weight who had retired early from the ring was the immediate impression the author made on his visitor. A round head, close-covered in curls, once fair but now pepper and salt; pale blue watchful eyes; a flat nose; expensive teeth; a silk handkerchief was wrapped with careful negligence round his short neck. Coat

and trousers were in contrasting shades of blue. His shoes
had cost too much.

Martin would describe the manner of his welcome as less
than genial, not allowing for the effect of his own approach
or Harper's sensible caution. A journalist is not by definition
an ally. And this one had the appearance of a hanging judge.

Inside, the house looked as if it had been arranged for the
shooting of a film epic; Harper led the way through Corin-
thian columns into a library, a delightful room, with french
windows opening out on to a lawn on which three handsome
children were playing with a quite lovely young woman.
Harper arranged two easy-chairs to embrace the view. Then
he invited Martin to drink. Comfortably seated, tumbler in
hand, absorbing the scene (the mountain was in the background), Martin was beginning to reconcile himself to the
afternoon when Harper said, "I like it here." He would
vulgarise the Day of Judgement. Martin had briefed himself
with routine questions; and soon he felt confident that even if
he were to doze during it he could reproduce a convincing
pastiche of the inevitable patter.

"Basically, I suppose I am a socialist. I don't know what
has happened to England. I'm afraid the people have lost
their nerve. Over here I get the feeling that you have managed to hold on to what they are throwing away at home.
Perhaps it's a question of priorities."

The girl was lying down, letting the children climb on top
of her. Martin glanced at Harper to show that he was still
listening when he realised that he was attending only to the
scene on the lawn. The author required no encouragement
to continue. He was on his favourite topic.

"I'm not a religious man, in the conventional sense of the
word, you understand. I don't belong to any kind of sect. I
see something to attract me in Buddhism, Zen, Taoism, the
Muslim faith—Christianity, if you will. I suppose in spite
of what I said just now I am basically religious. Shit!"

Mr Harper's tumbler had overturned. He mopped up and
refilled.

"What was I saying just now?"

"You said 'Shit'."

"I'll have to send these pants to the cleaners. LILY."

He called out very loud to attract the attention of the beautiful young woman who was bending down in an attractive attitude to succour one of the children, injured in their romp. She turned her face round in acknowledgement of the roar from the window.

"Remind me to send these pants to the cleaners." Harper was red from the exertion of shouting. He returned to Martin. "I don't think she heard. Where were we?"

"You had dealt with religion. I'm sure our readers would like to know your writing plans."

"I'm on a novel just now about a little Arab boy who has been adopted by a family in Israel. I got the idea when I was reading a book about T. E. Lawrence. That's someone I'd like to write a book about. Not a straight biography. I like to take someone real and historic and put him into a fictionalised situation. I always take care to get my background right. I spent six months in Israel. Shit!"

Mr Harper had upset his whiskey again.

"I'm not, basically, a literary man," he resumed. "I might never write another book when I finished this one. I don't have to. There's more in life than just writing. Shit!"

This time Martin was relieved to notice that nothing had been spilt.

The group outside on the grass was breaking up.

"I'd like to meet your wife," Martin said.

"I don't know where she is. I expect she will be back in time for dinner. I say, will you stay and have dinner with us? You haven't got to rush away, have you?"

Martin hesitated.

"That's settled then. Here, fill up." He poured whiskey with a lavish hand.

"You have lovely children," Martin said.

"Yes. They are. Basically, you might say, I'm a family man."

The children had scattered in one direction; the young woman came away from them towards the men. She seemed to be unaware of their attention.

"How did it go?" Harper said when she came in.

"That's a silly question." Her voice might have been American, or she was using a lingua franca to obscure her accent of origin.

"Oh, it's a silly question, is it?" Harper said, caressing her.

"I want a cigarette," she said, shaking herself free.

"Richard is from the newspaper," Harper explained.

Martin looked up at this, but she appeared not to have heard. He might have been invisible. She sprawled in a chair and fingered a magazine. "Where's Laura?" she said suddenly.

"I don't know. I wonder what she has arranged for dinner."

To answer that, a van drove up, and a woman with a hard, handsome face got out, and slammed the door as if she was punishing it. Harper greeted her when she was within earshot.

"Hello, Laura. Richard is here from the newspaper. What are the prospects of dinner?"

Laura gave a short nod in Martin's direction.

"Bella's in season," the girl said.

"I told you that yesterday," Mrs Harper replied, and went indoors.

In spite of the air of reluctance which preceded it, dinner, when it came, was lavish. A boy with a homely, local face appeared from nowhere and served at table. Harper carved. This was something he obviously liked to do, that he did well. It should on no account be overlooked. Martin took a note.

Mrs Harper sat looking at her plate, apparently oblivious to her surroundings. The girl made a vague effort to help, but mostly concentrated on a whitlow that had appeared on her finger. She showed it to Mrs Harper.

"I wouldn't suck it if I were you," she said without looking up.

With the carving done, Harper settled down and began to describe for Martin's benefit places he had visited, and Martin had lived in.

"The trouble with Australia," Harper began.

"When the British left Burma . . ."

"I saw it coming in Singapore . . ."

But Martin had taken as much from this facile ass as he was prepared to swallow. He had listened to his ramblings about politics, ethics, philosophy; he had still to find out certain facts about him; he was not going to be told about places in which he had spent a third of his life and Harper had only descended upon to find backdrops for his mechanised plots and pasteboard characters. However, Harper was not to be thwarted in this way. When Martin refused to listen, he turned to the girl, and raised his voice. Having abandoned the whitlow to its fate, she was giving her finger-nails a routine inspection. Mrs Harper, when she wasn't eating or drinking, was absorbed in the reflection at the bottom of her glass. Martin's presence, it was pretty clear, had made no alteration in the dinner routine. He was merely one more in a captive audience. When the boy was in the room, Harper sometimes addressed him (he had been given a summary of the incidence of cancer in the Philippines when he was removing the soup bowls).

Having stood in the way, as it were, whenever Harper tried to disembark at ports east of Suez, Martin was not less determined that he should not have to sit and listen to this charlatan shooting his line when it came to the discussing of books. When the fellow began to quote poetry ancient and modern in long mouthfuls Martin, who had no facility for learning by heart, failed to conceal his irritation. He might have been a gamekeeper who had spied a trespasser in his lord's demesne. Harper refused to respond to the signals, but he saw them, and he knew that Martin was feeling hard done by and envious; he recognised that superior tone, and he knew how much it was worth. He watched Martin undressing Lily with his eyes, and he enjoyed his failure to make any impression on her. Martin's unrealised pretensions made him a very suitable choice for an interviewer—that editor knew his job. If he had not been a failure the fellow would not be doing hackwork for a newspaper. Let him give himself airs; he was impressing nobody. What mattered was to keep out of a row and get this interview into a satisfactory shape. Harper didn't want for advertisement. The story would be of more value to the newspaper than it would be to him. But he was concerned about what he called his *persona*. He was obsessed by the phenomenon that he was, and anxious that the public should get the right picture. A failure, working off his grudge, could distort the perspective; and one could never be sure that a lie might not become a legend; the more obscure the origin of the lie, the more difficult it was to nail it.

Harper was not going to be bullied by Martin; neither was he going to quarrel with him. It would be stupid. He even asked Martin a few questions about himself. Was he married? Yes. Had he children? Three. Was his wife Irish? No. Had he met her abroad? Yes. But he avoided asking him about his own writing. That would extend disproportionately an exactly calculated concession. Harper had a few simple guide rules. One of these was always to be the only author in the room. Pulling in the line, he returned to books. He had been absorbed in Pepys recently. Had Martin ever read Pepys's diary?

"When I was a boy at school."

But the sarcasm miscarried.

"Then you haven't read the recent edition. My God, that gives you an insight into human nature."

Mrs Harper got up, went to the sideboard, took up a bottle, and returned with it to her place.

"You may say what you like but the whole of Proust is contained in that episode with Deb. Do you agree?"

Martin tried to sit out the question; when he saw from the other's fixed expression that this wasn't going to work, he said, "I can't for the moment . . ."

"Tell me who has put it better."

"Put what better?"

"Man's principal obsession; it's the core of every love story since the world began."

"I never thought of Pepys ..."

Martin couldn't go on. His opponent had all the ammunition. He had had to cede ground on three Shakespearian quotations earlier in the evening. How much longer was he going to have to stand this torture? But Harper was satisfied. He was too full of his subject to waste time rubbing his victory in.

"Deb was the maid—his wife's maid. When they were pretty he used to make passes at them. Mrs Pepys caught him at it when Deb was combing nits out of his hair. The girl was sent packing; Mrs P went at her lord with the tongs. They were red hot. She meant business. But that is not what is important. Pepys being a good-hearted man was sorry he had been the means of getting the girl sacked and injuring her reputation. He was miserable about the hurt to his marriage. He didn't want to shake it. He was a great upholder of convention—the archetypal civil servant. He was sorry for his long-suffering wife, and mad because from now on she would watch every step of his wanton way. But what to do you think upset him most? What at the moment he describes as the most wretched in his life pressed on his mind until he was almost mad? I'll tell you: *the fact that he hadn't collected the girl's maidenhead*."

Mrs Harper, who had been gazing into the bottom of her empty glass, filled it up again: the girl, Lily, lit a cigarette and followed the spiralling ascent of the smoke through half-closed eyes. Harper, having delivered the knock-out blow, stared at Martin to see what effect it had had on him.

He had not been impressed. He refused to be bullied by this bore. "Is that so?"

"It bloody well is. Does it surprise you?"

"Pepys was rather lecherous, wasn't he? In a rather shame-faced sort of way."

"Pepys was your average man. That's his claim to fame.

Tell me, if you had to choose, would you prefer your woman to have had someone else before you or after you?"

Martin glanced at their companions. Neither of them seemed aware of his presence. Mrs Harper was confiding her thoughts to her glass; Lily was staring at Harper through a curtain of smoke.

"I can't see the point of that question," Martin said. He was beginning to feel angry again.

"It is the most fundamental question in the world. Every man has asked it who has ever been in love."

"Nonsense."

"Every man who had the virility of a whelk, that is."

"I refuse to believe no bride is a virgin or fidelity is a thing of the past."

"But how can you *know*?"

"Well . . ." Martin looked at the women and then shrugged his shoulders. He was not going to let this vulgarian drag him into intimacy. And he caught an unpleasant whiff of that intent. Harper had been drinking steadily since Martin arrived. So had Martin.

"I'll tell you a story," Harper said, "and perhaps that will explain my attitude. For I don't make any bones about the fact that so long as I'm sure I'm the first, I don't give a damn who comes after me."

Mrs Harper stood up suddenly. "I'm going to water the horses," she said to the room as she left it. Martin took a covert glance at the girl. She seemed to be asleep. Harper looked as if he was hypnotised. On he rambled.

"I told you I was in Singapore for three months. I was getting the atmosphere and background for my first book, *The Yellow Moon*. Not my best, but a damn good story, though I says it myself. Shit. I met a girl there; just come out of a convent. She had the beauty of youth and a head of the most stunning flame-coloured hair. I've never in all my days seen such marvellous hair. We fell in love. I don't think either of us gave much thought to the future. We were young; we were happy. We lived for each day. I asked her to marry me.

I was married at the time, and it meant waiting for a divorce and all the rest of it. But I think she would have taken a chance if her father hadn't stepped in—a miserable old bugger—and forbade her to leave. She was nineteen. She had no money of her own. And I had a wife. That was the set-up. It was too much for her. We spent the last day visiting all the sacred haunts—you've been in love yourself. You know the sort of thing. I'd never tried to touch her. I was sentimental in those days. If you had asked me I'd have told you that I had no intention of doing so. But when it came to the time to go, and I knew I might never see her again, I was damned if I was going to leave that flower for someone else to gather. It wasn't in my blood. The decision, you can understand, lay with me. That hair wasn't lying. There was a fire there. I am always right about these matters.

"I never heard what happened to her afterwards. I promised to write—you know how you do—but didn't, of course, and I met Laura later in the year. I dare say there were others who went the way I went; I feel no animus towards them. I got there first. You can't expect a woman to live all her life long on one throw. It wouldn't be fair."

She had told him after one of his jealous fits that there had been someone else; but only one, and only once. When she was in one of her silent moods he used to suspect her of brooding over that first lover. It was all so long ago, when her hair was a flame. Now the fire was out, and he would have said that he could no longer feel jealous. But he had met the man, and he would never forgive her. She had cheapened everything that they had had together; cheapened herself; and cheapened him.

> "I found you as a morsel cold
> Upon dead Caesar's platter."

Harper was quoting Shakespeare again, and looking pleased with himself. When it dawned on him that he was giving evidence against his own case, he said: "I'm sure Julius C would have agreed with me. Antony may have been a wonder man, but Caesar got in first. By the look on your face, I think I've convinced you. Here, your glass is empty."

Resisting simultaneously two violent and conflicting impulses, Martin allowed him to fill his glass; he had been employed to write a description of Harper; and as the wine poured into the glass the first paragraph began to form in his mind.